Tires screeched as Ronny slid the car around a corner, scraping the guardrail. Sparks flew. He righted the wheel and roared straight ahead. He was good.

A police siren wailed, and a cruiser tore out suddenly from a side road. A motorcycle cop drove right behind him. The tinny loudspeaker demanded that we pull over.

Ronny sped up.

If the Legion had been smart, or if they had cared, they would have split up and gone on their way. But they weren't smart. They were deadly. And the only things they cared about were getting that book and getting rid of me.

Whoever I was.

Look for these titles in
THE HAUNTING OF DEREK STONE series:

#1: City of the Dead

#2: Bayou Dogs

#3: The Red House

#4: The Ghost Road

THE GHOST ROAD

TONY ABBOTT

SCHOLASTIC INC.

NEW YORK TORONTO LONDON AUCKLAND
SYDNEY MEXICO CITY NEW DELHI HONG KONG

ISBN-13: 978-0-545-03432-6
ISBN-10: 0-545-03432-9

12 11 10 9 8 7 6 5 4 3 2 9 10 11 12 13 14/0

First printing, September 2009

To Those Who Can't Remain

CONTENTS

THE GHOST ROAD

ONE

Wild Hearses

After I finished throwing up, we started driving again.

My brother — Ronny — and Abby Donner were silent and tired as we tore up the foggy roads outside Coushatta. We'd been driving all night, and it was the third time I'd gotten sick in as many hours.

"Sorry," I mumbled, as I had the first two times. But I wasn't. Throwing up was my body's way of saying, "Nope. Can't digest this insanity. No way."

You'd chuck it all up too if, right out of the blue, someone told you — no, *hundreds* of people told you —

"You hear that?" Abby interrupted my thoughts.

Ronny tore his eyes from the rearview mirror and slowed the hearse. "What?"

"Shhh." I turned and looked out the back window. "I hear it, too. . . ."

Ronny pulled to the shoulder of the road near a stretch of weedy fence, flicked off the headlights, and cocked his head. "I don't hear anything. You guys are —"

Abby screamed, "A truck!"

Wrong. Three trucks, racing out of the fog behind us.

Ronny jammed his foot on the gas and spun the wheel. The hearse slid behind the fence, throwing me and Abby to the floor. Ronny jerked to a stop as the trucks shot past us, racing north toward Shreveport.

I couldn't see the faces of the drivers, but I could hear their voices — whining, angry, squealing, groaning. I knew who they were.

Dead men.

The trucks didn't slow down, just barreled up the road and out of sight. We had escaped. For now.

Ronny snorted. "Well, that could've been bad."

Abby climbed back into her seat and swatted him with the road map. She wasn't being playful. "Jerk! I don't want to rebreak my ankle! Why can't you just drive like a normal person?"

Ronny turned to her, his face suddenly cold. "You want reasons?"

That was a joke. Sort of.

Ronny wasn't a normal person. He was as dead as the men in those trucks.

That probably explained why he wasn't a great driver. But with the Legion after you, bad driving isn't such a big deal.

The Legion?

Man, I hope you've been listening to what I've already told you, because there's not much time for a big story.

Today it would all happen.

Ronny skidded the car — a beat-up 1954 Cadillac hearse about a block and a half long — back onto the road, and we drove on.

To start from the beginning, my name is Derek Stone. More about me later. What you really need to know now is that Ronny died a few weeks back in a train wreck. It happened at a place called Bordelon Gap on the Red River.

Abby and I were there, too. I was injured and Abby was in a coma for a month, but we're okay — more or less. Not Ronny. He was one of nine people who died. But he came back a few weeks later. In fact, all the crash victims came back, including my father and Abby's mother, Madeline Donner. None of them were themselves anymore, except maybe my dad. I wasn't sure about him.

How did they come back from the dead?

Through a thing called the Rift — or the

Wound — a tear in the fabric between this world and the next. The opening allowed dead souls to reanimate dying bodies, if the manner of death was the same. That's called translation.

Turns out — surprise! — the road to the afterlife is a two-way street.

Most of the victims were now inhabited by the souls of convicts who had died in an almost identical train crash at the same place in 1938. Except for Ronny, Abby's mom, and maybe my dad, the souls that returned were the advance troops of a huge dead army. The Legion.

The Legion's mission was simple: to bring their dead comrades back in huge numbers, to flood the land with evil, to destroy the living, and to spread their world of death here.

Not much. Just that.

Why do they want to come back? Ronny told me the land of the dead is a harsh place for evil souls — a world of perpetual torture. So over the centuries they banded together to fight the good souls. It's kind of like revenge. They want out of the afterlife.

They want to be back here.

Right now, the Legion's troops were driving north under the command of a guy named Erskine Cane. He was a murderer and arsonist, now in the body of a soldier. After translations at Bayou Malpierre (a creepy place where I nearly drowned when I was four) and Amaranthia (my mother's broken-down family home), the evil dead now numbered about two hundred fifty.

Translation is a really ugly thing. It's horrible, the way the dead soul forces its way into a dying body. A good soul would never translate unless it were absolutely necessary, unless there were no choice.

But the evil dead have lost whatever makes others good. So, they want to come back? They translate.

Erskine Cane had been calling the shots so far, but I knew that the Legion's overall leader was someone even more powerful. He was known only as the First, and he was planning something huge. My guess was that he was going to blast the Wound wide open.

And he was going to do it today.

How did I know that?

According to Abby's dead mother, my job was to find the First, and I had "one day only."

She told me that yesterday.

Nothing like running out of time to add some pressure.

"Ronny, will you slow down!" Abby burst out.

"Uh, no," he said. "It'll be dawn in an hour, and I'm pretty sure it was your dead mom who said —"

"Don't talk about her like that!" Abby shouted.

"Stuff it, and find a better road map," Ronny replied.

Yeah. They weren't getting along. Ronny was on edge like nobody's business. I knew one reason. He had a patch of gray flesh on his neck and chin that had been spreading by the hour.

He was decaying fast.

I'm still learning the rules, but I'm pretty sure it was happening because Ronny had been translated on land. I'd seen enough dead people by now to know that bodies translated in water weren't decaying as quickly. That was because the Wound was located in water – the Red River, to be exact, which bends across Louisiana from one corner to the other. Dead souls moved through the river from the Wound, then translated into the dying wherever they found them.

I'd discovered some of this in old books, some on the Internet, and some from the crazy people I'd met over the last few days.

Ronny told me a lot, too. The soul that returned in his body was a farm boy named Virgil Black, who had died in the 1938 crash. For seventy years, Virgil had been a soldier fighting the Legion in the afterlife. He was one of the good guys. Now that the Legion was here, I was glad to have him on my side.

"Derek, hurry up and read that thing," Ronny said. "We don't have forever."

"Cut Derek some slack, will you?" said Abby. "Just read it!"

Right. The voices of the dead weren't the only things crowding my brain. There was *The Ghost Road,* a fifty-page poem I'd discovered at Amaranthia. It had been scribbled in scratchy black ink during the Civil War by a young captain named Ulysses Longtemps.

He's . . . an ancestor of mine.

The poem describes how Ulysses witnessed the First's translation during Louisiana's Red River Campaign in 1864. Ulysses then discovered the Wound between our worlds and closed it. My mother told me that I was supposed to follow the poem, discover the Wound like he did, and seal it shut again.

Terrific. I didn't like poems, did everything I could not to read them in school, and here I had to read a very long one in order to save the world.

My mother also said *The Ghost Road* was written in a kind of code — one that only I could understand. It's like Waldo Fouks, that creepy boy I met in the bayou, told me: I'm special.

It was a poem and it was written in code. Two big strikes against it, in my opinion.

Or maybe three. The poem wasn't even complete. I'd flipped to the end only to discover that the poem stopped abruptly in the middle of a line. Of course it did. Ulysses had died before he could finish it.

I'd found the book a few hours ago, but I'd barely had a chance to read it, never mind try to understand it. But holding it in my hands was like holding a living thing, somehow. Like cradling a beating heart.

Ronny swung his head around. "Anything?"

"I'm still looking," I said.

"Look faster."

When I opened to the first page of the poem, I saw the title inked in slanting black letters. A slash of rusty red ran from the bottom left corner to the upper right corner. It was a single stripe of color, a stain, blood soaked into the fibers of the page. It had become part of the poem it had seeped into.

I thought of the phrase "written in blood."

Whatever *The Ghost Road* was, the Legion wanted it. They wanted me, I knew. But they also wanted that book — wrinkled pages, bloodstain, and all.

Ronny slowed the hearse as we came to a crossroads. A lone stop sign was stuck in the ground, tilted severely away from the road. It looked like someone had crashed into it.

Ronny snickered. "Okay, now what?"

"Derek, can you read the words again?" Abby asked, scanning the map by the dim dashboard light.

It was dark in the car, but I found the lines of the poem that seemed to describe the place we were looking for. I read them aloud.

"'The river bends like weeping willow limbs

And there I thought I saw a widow bend to her dead love,

And saw his body bending in the tangled swamp.'"

"Lots of bending going on," said Ronny coolly.

I didn't read them the next line, though I couldn't get it out of my mind.

By end of day, I knew that dead love might be me.

"There's a place called Cemetery Bend coming up in a few miles," said Abby, tracing her finger across the map. "It's on the river, and there's a cross marked here. Do you think —"

"More than you do," Ronny cut in. The engine growled as he raced off again, burning rubber.

Abby sulked. "You waste gas every time you do that."

"So do you, when you open your mouth," Ronny muttered.

"Well, at least *I'm* not decaying," Abby said.

"Shut up!" I cried. "And pull over!"

Ronny braked fast, and I jumped out of the car, feeling my stomach flip over again. But it wasn't their arguing that was making me sick.

In Ulysses Longtemps's old room at Amaranthia,

among a chorus of weeping widows and the smell of magnolia, my mother had told me a terrible secret.

Leaning away from the hearse, spilling what was left of my guts onto the ground, I remembered every word and wondered what kind of hearse had carried me when I had died.

TWO

Hello-I-Must-Be-Going

When I had died.

If I actually believed what my mother told me in that dusty room at Amaranthia, I hadn't *nearly* drowned in that filthy bayou when I was four. I'd just plain drowned.

Not only that, but at the instant I drowned, I was translated.

That's right.

I was reanimated by the soul of the old poet captain, Ulysses Longtemps. Why? Because the world needed him more than me. After all, I was no one, but Ulysses Longtemps had closed the Wound.

In other words, since I was four I haven't been quite myself. I've been him.

It's like this:

Hi, I'm Derek Stone. I've been dead most of my life.

Or this:

Hi, I'm Derek. My next birthday is a hundred and fifty years ago.

You can't imagine the mess in my head right now. Derek Stone. Ulysses Longtemps. Old ghosts. The evil Legion.

Everyone trying to get a word in.

Abby didn't know about it yet. Poor Abby. Just a nice girl holding a cheesecake when I first saw her on that train. It seemed like a hundred lifetimes ago. Ronny didn't know who I really was, either, but I wondered how long it would take him to guess. He was a fellow dead guy, after all.

I hadn't figured out how to tell them. I couldn't believe it myself.

Except that I'd looked at it from every angle I could think of, and my being dead was the only thing that made sense. I saw dead people. I heard their voices. I could chat with ghosts. I understood things about Ulysses Longtemps that I couldn't possibly have known otherwise. I'd remembered bits of his poem long before I had ever seen that old book.

"Here." Abby handed me a paper towel through the car window.

I wiped my mouth and got back in.

Trees flashed by. Abby murmured something about the map. Ronny muttered behind the wheel and kept driving.

I knew that it was up to me to find Cemetery Bend and the Wound between life and death.

Ulysses had translated into me for that exact reason. As my mother had told me: *Safeguard your book with your life. Lose it, and we lose the war. Decipher it, follow its directions, and the Legion will fall, the Wound will be closed, and life can return.*

I only had one day to close the Wound, and if I couldn't follow the directions in the poem, things would get really nasty — really quickly. Ulysses' poem said:

> *. . . dark souls will flood the darkened earth from every drop of dark water . . .*

Lots of darkness going on.

"I thought you guys could hear the dead," Abby said, her eyes fixed on the rearview mirror. "The Legion's back!"

I swiveled in my seat and looked back at the curving road.

Headlights glowed in the fog behind us. I counted four distinct pairs of lights, but there were probably more. The drivers' screeching echoed in my ears now. I'd been so wrapped up in my thoughts that I hadn't heard the dead. But Ronny hadn't heard them, either. Why not?

"Lose them," I said.

Ronny scoffed. "This is what I was born for!"

That was true. Virgil Black used to race tractors back in Shongaloo when he was alive.

Ronny slammed his foot on the gas, and we pulled ahead. The voices of the dead shrieked in my bad ear, and the trucks didn't hang back. The front one sped up so quickly it rammed our bumper.

Tires screeched as Ronny slid the car around a corner, scraping the guardrail. Sparks flew. He righted the wheel and roared straight ahead. He was good.

A police siren wailed, and a cruiser tore out suddenly from a side road. A motorcycle cop drove right behind the cruiser. The tinny loudspeaker demanded that we pull over.

Ronny sped up.

If the Legion had been smart, or if they had cared, they would have split up and gone on their way. But they weren't smart. They were deadly. And the only things they cared about were getting that book and getting rid of me.

Whoever I was.

As we raced along a stretch of rain-flooded road, I saw the first truck behind us slow down to let the motorcycle and cruiser pull closer. As they did, the truck driver braked suddenly. The motorcycle rear-ended the truck, sending its driver flying into the woods by the side of the road. A second truck tore out of the fog and rammed the police car into the back of the first truck. It was sandwiched. Two other trucks pulled up around it and shrieked to a stop.

I wanted to look away — but I couldn't. Through the back window, I saw dead men throw the cruiser doors open and descend on the police, rolling them onto the flooded shoulder.

"No," I said. "Another translation?"

"Are we just going to leave —" Abby started.

"You can stay," said Ronny. "I'm getting out of here!"

We raced up the road, and fog surrounded us again. I turned in my seat and stared blankly out the front window of the hearse. No use looking back now. The cops were goners.

"Those poor men," said Abby quietly.

"Better them than us," said Ronny. "Read the map."

Abby shook her head but said nothing.

There was nothing to say. Death surrounded us. All we could do was keep it from getting too close.

Then it surrounded us for real.

Something flashed by the window on my right. It matched the speed of the hearse, even as we went faster. I edged my eyes toward it, not wanting to see. A face — white — dead, flying through the fog outside the car.

I turned away. "No. Please."

"What?" asked Abby, turning in her seat to look at me.

I shut my eyes tight. When I opened them, I saw a

second face speeding through the fog on the other side of the hearse. It spoke.

We're ready. Lead us.

"No . . ."

The first face repeated it. *We're ready!*

I glanced at Ronny in the rearview mirror. His eyes were set on the road ahead.

Why didn't he hear the voices or see the faces? What was wrong with him? If he was dead, like me, why couldn't he hear the ghosts? He always used to!

Suddenly, they were in the backseat with me.

Two ghosts in old uniforms — the Rebel uniforms I had seen on the ghosts at Amaranthia. They had ashen skin, hard black eyes. They pointed out the window to my right.

There . . . there!

"What? Right?" I said. "Turn right?"

The ghosts wailed. *There!*

"Turn right!" I cried.

"Are you kidding?" said Ronny. "It's just woods."

"We're still three miles from Cemetery Bend," Abby added.

"Turn! Now!" I shouted.

Ronny jerked the wheel fast. The ghosts vanished with a shriek as we bounced off the road and into the woods.

"Ronny, slow down!" Abby shouted.

I hit the ceiling and crumpled back down to the seat. Abby fell to the floor again. We struck a stump. I heard the rear bumper rip off. We banged and nicked trees one after another until a bright light burst through the branches and blinded us.

"What –" Ronny cried. He slammed on the brakes.

A man jumped out of the trees in front of us, holding a musket. "Halt!"

I screamed.

THREE

Night Work

"Stop screaming!" Ronny spat as the hearse slid to a stop on the pine needles. "What are you, two years old?"

When he shut off the engine, it was eerily quiet. The fierce light vanished. A musty smell suddenly seeped through the windows.

"Y'all okay in there?"

Leaning toward the car was a late-middle-aged man with fat rosy cheeks, a squat hat pulled low over his forehead, and a beard like a shag rug hanging from ear to ear. He looked like an out-of-work Santa — except that he wore a uniform of filthy mustard-colored wool and carried an old musket.

"Y'all okay?" he repeated, squinting into the car.

Abby drew in a quick breath. "Did we, like, take a wrong turn and come out a hundred years ago?"

Santa laughed. "A hundred and forty-four! This is April of 1864. You musta gotten the e-mail!"

Great. Just what we needed — more crazy.

"Another hour and you would have missed the big battle," he added.

"Battle?" Ronny said. "Between who?"

"Depends," Santa said, leaning on the car. "You a Mouton or a Taylor? Taylors are right about here. Mouton's men are gathering west of Swamp Road." He paused to chuckle. "They call it Swamp Road on account of some days it's one, some days it's the other. Wagons are coming soon, if you want to hitch a ride. Beauchamp's men haven't arrived at all yet."

Ronny turned to us. "Who's crazy here, him or me?"

I couldn't process it, either, until I remembered that Taylor, Beauchamp, and Mouton were names of Confederate commanders during the Civil War.

"Wait a second," I said. "Is there going to be a . . ." I couldn't think of the word. "A . . . reenactment of a battle?"

"Why, yessir!" Santa said, eyeing Ronny's darkening neck and scratching his own. "Largest gathering of what we call 'living historians' ever. Five thousand soldiers, fifteen hundred horses, a thousand wagons. Starts this morning at dawn."

The man couldn't seem to come up with a complete sentence.

Abby turned to me. "Why didn't we know about this?"

"Maybe we've been a little out of touch?" I said, climbing out of the hearse.

I glanced around and realized that my heart was pounding like a hammer on an anvil. I had never been there before . . . right?

We were completely surrounded by woods, but I somehow knew what lay beyond them — undulating hillocks and channels, all bunched up here and there like a wrinkled carpet. There was a long field, sloping downward from the road to the river. Thick woods bordered it on either side, along with sodden ditches, swamps, stone walls, and rocky outcroppings. A nightmare of a battlefield. And I knew every inch of it.

'Twas there we massed, that swamp upon a swamp . . .

"Is this Cemetery Bend?" I asked no one in particular.

"Abba-solutely, son," said Santa, flicking his eyes to the sky. The guy liked to talk. "Skirmish at the crest of Bloody Meadow comes at first light, 'bout an hour. You'll need to get your car out of here. We're in 1864, remember."

I *did* remember. It was almost like reading the lines right off the page.

. . . blue-clad invaders drove their wagons up the road,
While graybacks we, we massed our steeds,
Our thoughts all haunted by what lay ahead.

My heart sank. I didn't know exactly what lay ahead, but I was sure none of it was going to be good.

The bright light flashed over us again.

"What *is* that?" Abby asked, climbing out of the car and standing next to me. Ronny stayed put behind the wheel.

Santa moved a few paces away, then cleared his throat and swung his musket out toward the woods. As the light moved on, we could see what looked like a big river barge just off the nearest bank. It was a flatboat with a large cabin at one end. Cranes and shovels were digging at the water from the flat part of the barge.

"Night work on the river," the pretend soldier said. "That there is a dredger. Deepens the river at this point every ten years or so. River clogs with silt and dirt. Dredgers drag it out from Shreveport all the way down to Bordelon, where it gets too narrow."

The name rushed through my veins like ice. Bordelon. Where our train had crashed. Where Ronny had been translated. Where I had begun to hear the dead.

"Dicky Meade owns the dredger. He promised to go quiet for the reenactment," Santa continued. "Battle ends with fireworks from his boat at dusk. His boat's gonna be our teakettle!"

That sparked something in me.

While silent pass the teakettles, breathing steam and rage,
The phantom comes, the phantom goes.

Talk about code. The phantom?

"Teakettle?" said Abby. "Um . . . what?"

Two men in similar dirty uniforms joined the first one. They glanced up and down the length of our hearse and grinned, each showing a set of yellow teeth.

One of the men sighed. "You folks need to be educated. A teakettle's a ship! Federal ironclad, with iron plates on the outside. Teakettle. Get it?"

Ronny drummed his fingers loudly on the steering wheel. "Are we done here?"

"No," I said, turning back to the reenactors. "Tell me about the teakettles."

Santa looked delighted to "educate" the city folk.

"The big kettle in the campaign was a Union gunboat called the *Eastport*," he said. "The captain scuttled it — sank it — rather than let it fall into Rebel hands. Because it was a munitions boat, it blew up something fierce, and kept exploding under the water. Flooded the banks of Cemetery Bend during the battle, all the way up to Swamp Road. There'll be fireworks at dusk, meant to represent the scuttling of the *Eastport*. Dicky Meade is pulling out all the stops —"

Before he could finish, the sky opened up.

"Dang!" said Santa, hunching his shoulders and turning his face up to the rain. "Now we're gonna be mud fighting. And here come the wagons —"

Abby and I jumped back into the car. From my half-open window, I smelled horses. The squeal of wooden wheels and the shouting of men echoed nearby.

Rain pooled quickly in the grass and on the old road behind us. Within minutes, it was a torrent, coming cold and heavy. Men lurched among the trees in bunches, all calling and yelling.

"Cemetery Bend is already a swamp," Santa barked through the car window, shielding his face with his arm. "In this rain, there could be lots of friendly fire. Thank goodness these guns don't actually shoot. Five thousand come to battle, five thousand fight, and five thousand go home safe and sound!"

Abby turned to me. I knew we were thinking the same thing. Five thousand might come and fight, but they wouldn't all go home safe and sound.

The Legion was coming.

Still, was there something else about the teakettle and the fireworks? Something had clicked in my brain. I just wasn't sure what. Santa said that the

Eastport was a munitions boat that had exploded under the water.

Was that how the Wound had opened in the first place?

I suddenly felt dumb. Why couldn't I understand anything? Thanks to the ghosts, we had found Cemetery Bend. But now what? Time was running out. I had to decipher the code.

"Back your hearse to Swamp Road," Santa yelled through the downpour, pointing his musket the way we'd come. "There's parking in the far field." He turned and hustled off with the yellow-teeth men.

We rolled the windows closed.

"Men didn't play with guns in my day," Ronny muttered.

"Should we tell them we think something's going to happen?" asked Abby. "The Legion and everything?"

"They would never believe it," said Ronny. "But you can bet this battlefield is where it will happen, so it's where we need to be. You stay here. I'll park the car and be back."

I felt hopelessness almost crush me as Abby and I stepped out into the rain. The reenactment *was* the perfect cover for a mass translation. Five thousand men — fresh bodies — at the site of a battle on the Red River.

But how would it happen?

How could we get anyone to believe us?

And how could we possibly stop it?

FOUR

Flooded Ditches

Abby and I followed a small group of "soldiers" to a campfire in the woods.

Some men huddled under cloaks. Some stood under trees, laughing, their uniforms already soaked through. "Realistic!" I heard one say.

He was right. It had rained during the original battle of Cemetery Bend, too. I can't say how I knew that.

About a dozen men crouched around the hissing fire, including Santa and his yellow-teeth friends. They had hung a canvas sheet between some trees to protect them from the drenching rain. The shelter collected smoke, but the men didn't seem to mind. They flapped the edge of the canvas, inviting us in, and Abby scampered underneath.

"Maybe today's not a good day for a battle," Abby said to the men, giving me a look.

"Because of the rain?" one of the yellow-teeth guys scoffed. "Rain don't stop soldiers."

"But it makes everything more dangerous," I put in. "People could die today. I mean for real."

The yellow-teeth men both looked at me at the same time. It was almost like they were connected. "What exactly are you trying to say, son?" one of them asked while the other scratched his head.

How to answer?

I took the plunge. What was the worst that could happen?

"The dead are coming. Hundreds of them —"

"Wooo-hooo!" said the other yellow-teeth man, grinning. "You got some kind of screw loose." He turned to Abby. "See to your boyfriend, miss. He's crazy!"

"He's not . . . my boyfriend," Abby said. I thought she might be blushing.

"You saying he *is* crazy, then?" Santa said.

The soldiers laughed.

Yeah, hilarious.

"Derek, just let it go," Abby whispered. "Let's wait for Ronny."

She was right. The whole dead-coming-back thing sounded insane when you just came out with it; I knew that. I was about to sit down next to Abby when I spotted a reenactor standing in the rain a few feet away. He wasn't much older than Ronny, and he was so thin that I almost hadn't seen him at all.

"Hey," I called.

His eyes flicked toward me, then away. His hair — blond, filthy, soaked, and matted — stuck out below the edges of his cap. He held a pistol in one hand, its barrel pointing to the ground. His legs were bowed, as if he had grown up riding horses. His boots were torn and ragged, and his trousers were ripped. I had to admit that it was an authentic look for a young kid.

"Come under the tent," I said. "There's room —"

Abby looked up at me. So did three of the men around the fire.

"You'll be leaving us soon," the young soldier said to me.

I shrugged. "Maybe."

What difference did that make?

"Maybe what?" Santa asked.

"Maybe we'll be leaving," I said.

"No problem," one of the yellow-teeth men said. "There's still an hour before dawn. Reporters just left. You might have a bit of trouble getting past the police cordon, though. Because of the rain, the fields are sure to flood. They'll want to keep civilians back behind the line."

"You'll be leaving soon," the boy said again.

"What's your name?" I asked him.

“Frank,” an older guy crouching next to the fire responded. He looked up at me. But I wasn’t talking to him.

“Jeremiah Ross,” said the boy, still looking away. His voice was faint, maybe from yelling. “Folks call me Jem. You know that. Or maybe you forgot. Time on the battlefield does things to your head.”

That made me think he had actually fought in a real battle, not just weekend reenactments.

“Okay . . . ,” I said softly, stepping toward him. I was getting rained on, but I didn’t care.

Abby rose. “Derek?”

“You start seeing things,” the young man continued. “Can’t sleep, can’t sit, can’t stand, your head aches, your heart aches from dawn to dark to dawn again until heat rips your side, and you fall, and there is only gray. . . .”

He drifted off. His words were beautiful, but nutty. It seemed like he was in some kind of trance.

“But if it’s not fun, why do you do it?” I said to him.

“Oh, it’s fun,” Frank piped up. “It’s plenty fun. A weekend away from the wives! Get under the tarp, kid.” He gestured to me.

“Fun?” Jem replied. “I saw my brother take a musket shot to the neck. Died in a ditch. They all died in ditches." He shrugged and spat on the ground.

"Sorry," I said, flinching. I paused for a minute. "Why don't you come under the tent?"

"Who?" Frank asked.

"Derek?" Abby whispered. "Are you okay?"

I stared at Jem. "Come on under the tent."

"No. I've got to show you some things." He finally turned his face to the firelight.

Half of it wasn't there. Jem's right cheek and half his lips were gone.

I must have made a noise.

"Derek?" said Abby, walking out into the rain and putting her hand on my arm. She nearly stepped on the boy's foot.

Jem squinted at her. "That girl shouldn't be here. This is going to get ugly."

"Derek, are you all right?" Abby asked.

"Captain, come with me," said Jem.

That's when I knew.

No one saw the young soldier but me.

FIVE

From the Tower

As soon as I realized Jem was a ghost, I could see the obvious signs that I'd missed. Rain was pouring right through him, splashing on the ground below as if he wasn't there at all.

"I've got to show you some things," he repeated.

His eyes were black marbles, boring into mine. He didn't blink at all. Then he walked off through the rain. I glanced back at Abby and saw Ronny picking through the woods toward us. I turned away from them.

"Derek, wait," Abby said.

I didn't.

"Ronny, hurry," Abby called. "Derek's seeing someone."

Frank hooted. "Must make you jealous!"

Jem was already deep in the trees. I ran after him.

In a clearing ahead stood a tall, square rough-log structure — an observation tower. The top, which was fifty or so feet high, was a roofed and railed platform above the treetops. Wooden stairs zig-zagged from the base up.

Without pausing to look for me, Jem stumbled onto the stairs and began to climb. I was out of breath by the time I reached the top. You'd think I'd have been in better shape after all the running from the dead I'd been doing.

In the corner of the platform, a short kid about the same age as Ronny was sitting on a little stool made of logs. He wore a park uniform shirt and a name tag that said *Chad*. He flicked his eyes up from his iPod when I got up there.

He sighed and stood. "Ooh, a visitor. Lucky me. So the rain didn't keep you away, like everyone else?"

Of course, the kid didn't see Jem there with us.

Sighing to himself, Chad popped one earbud out and launched into his little memorized speech.

"Welcome to the official observation post of the Cemetery Bend Memorial Battlefield. I'm one of several guides you may meet during today's reenactment. This tower was erected in 1964 on the hundredth anniversary of the Civil War Battle of Cemetery Bend. It also acts as a bell tower for official battlefield events. You'll hear the bell ring in a little while."

He motioned mechanically to a thick rope that hung from the top of the roof and passed through a hole in the floor to the ground.

The guy droned on, bored by his own words. Chad reminded me of how Ronny used to be, before he died.

As I only half-listened, I got my first good look at the battlefield through the mist and smoke. It was several square miles, centered on Bloody Meadow, a wrinkled landscape of channels and bumps that were riddled with flooding ditches. The meadow bent first one way, then another, from Swamp Road all the way down to the riverbank.

I saw the gray stones of a cemetery in the woods below. A little distance away was a long, low building, like a stable. On the near side of the meadow, between the tower and the cemetery, stood a big barn. It leaned away from the wagon path, like it might topple at any minute.

It was hard to look at the field without feeling like I knew it. *Really* knew it. In my mind I saw men charging across the meadow from different angles, heard their shouts mix with the blasts of weapons. Two and a half thousand had died before the Battle of Cemetery Bend was over.

"The foot of Bloody Meadow," Jem said to me,

pointing to where the rutted field met the river. "Too many died there. That's where Beauchamp's Butchers were killed."

"What?" I said.

Chad stopped his spiel. "*What* what?" He looked at me impatiently.

"Beauchamp's Butchers," I said.

"Butchers?" another voice chimed in. Ronny had reached the top of the tower. He wasn't nearly as out of breath as I'd been. "Sounds about right. What did they do?"

The guide didn't seem interested in Ronny's appearance. He riffled lazily through his brochure. "There's not much here. I remember people saying that Clarence Beauchamp was a nutcase, but had, like, this loyalty thing with his troops. He went berserk on the battlefield, killing civilians — anyone he thought was helping the Yankees take Cemetery Bend."

Jem's eyes drifted to the riverbank at the foot of the meadow. "The other troops pushed them into the river after they mutinied at the height of the battle. A massacre, some say."

"What happened to Beauchamp?" I asked.

"Some other general led his troops against Beauchamp's. Finally had to kill them all. In the water. It's what ended the battle." Chad's eyes widened. It was the first time he'd looked anything but indifferent. "They say their ghosts still haunt the cemetery. A couple thousand creepy killers. It was insane, dude."

Abby finally appeared and leaned on the railing, slowly rotating her ankle. "Sorry. It still hurts."

Jem shook his head. "She shouldn't be here."

"You're s-s-seeing somebody, aren't you?" Ronny whispered to me. "But I can't. How is th-th-that possible?"

Was Ronny stuttering now? Or was it just the cold rain? I tried to ignore it and turned back to Chad. "People are going to die here today. You should go home."

He laughed. "Not me. I get paid by the hour. Plus, the rain is keeping most tourists away. No prob for me. I still get paid."

"Ask him about that thing," Jem said, nodding toward the dredging barge.

I did. The guide peered toward the river.

"I don't know," he said. "Hold on." He shuffled noisily through his brochure again, clearly annoyed at having to do what he was getting paid for.

"The dredging started ten years ago, when I was, like, seven," he said absentmindedly. "In Shreveport, then on south. Here it is." He read from the brochure. "'Arriving at this part of the river a decade ago, the dredging company discovered massive ledges of bedrock beneath the accumulated silt. They realized that in order to increase the underwater area, they would have to detonate explosives in the river bed. A series of powerful explosions disturbed enough of the bedrock to effectively deepen the river.' "

"Ten y-years ago?" said Ronny, giving me the eye. "Not exactly a surprise, is it?"

My mind raced. If the Wound was somewhere in the riverbed, had it first opened when the *Eastport* was destroyed in 1864? And had it opened again when the bedrock was detonated ten years ago to dredge the river? Could the two explosions have been so sudden and so massive that they'd ripped the veil?

I looked out at the dredger, which was nearly motionless in the river.

I knew, of course, that the afterlife wasn't exactly a geographic location. It wasn't that simple or that physical. But the separation between us and the afterlife must have been something, after all. A kind of veil between the living world and the land of the dead that you couldn't see or feel but was still there.

It reminded me of a passage from a book I'd read when this whole thing began. *Afterlives* by Tomas Deak had convinced me that translation was possible.

A ghost is a mere shadow, like the shadow cast from a distant object. That shadow can be seen in our world from time to time — as in a "haunting." But the distant object from which it is cast is its soul. After death, the soul resides exclusively in the afterlife — unless it returns in physical form.

I knew that. Ghosts pass through the veil all the time without there being an actual hole. But the Wound was different. It must be where the veil between the worlds was weakest. It was something like a rip, a tear, but so small that only one soul could pass through it at a time. *Afterlives* went on:

. . . it is speculated that when the veil between the worlds of life and death breaks open — a sort of rip in the fabric — souls may be able to transport into dying bodies if the manner of death is the same. The more similar the manner of death, the better the fit.

That would explain why there had been so few translations. I'd read that passage what felt like ages ago. Was I finally beginning to understand?

Lights flashed from the river. I heard the clanking and grinding of cranes. The dredging had started up again.

"A bridge," Abby suddenly said, pointing.

On the northern edge of the battleground was a long stone bridge with seven arches built over a flowing tributary of the Red River.

"Long Bridge," said Chad. "There was a skirmish there at about dusk the first day of battle. The Long Bridge Skirmish. Hundreds of cavalry were killed."

"You probably don't want to remember what happened there," said Jem quietly, peering at me. "But I think you've got to, Captain."

And suddenly I *did* remember. The Long Bridge Skirmish wasn't a skirmish at all. It was a massacre. And Ulysses' men were the victims. Close to four hundred cavalry troops were ambushed there by Yankee guerrillas.

I snapped open the old cartridge box that held Ulysses' book and found the right lines.

Chains meant to bind, tore hooves asunder. We charged
Across the bridge. A few of us — no more — passed by
Before those chains pulled taut across the stone,
And sent both horse and man to ambush and to
death below.

But that was poetry. I also remembered — really remembered — the mayhem on the stones. The shots. The sudden attack. Sabers hacking. Rain. Blood. Confusion.

I shook.

Abby put her hand on my arm. "Derek —"

Jem motioned upriver. "That's the most important thing I need to show you. Your manufactory. That phantom took you away."

Okay, my mind was reeling with enough stuff — totally, completely unbelievable stuff — and now that word again: "phantom."

Following Jem's gaze, I saw a squat building of blackened brick hugging the shore a couple of miles up the river. It was barely visible in the driving rain.

"We're ready to fight," Jem said slowly, his voice sounding through the open hole in his cheek. I couldn't help shuddering. "Hundreds will follow you to close the Wound and stop the Grand Return."

Jem didn't have to tell me what the Grand Return was. Looking down on the sodden fields, I could imagine it just fine. A huge translation. *The* huge translation.

I didn't have time to get too carried away before a crazy reenactor rode a horse like a banshee through the woods below, calling the men to the first reenacted skirmish. The fake soldiers cheered.

"Oh, right. My other job," the guide muttered. He loped to the nearby rope and gave it a tug. The bell clanged overhead.

Dawn? Already? But it was still as gray as night.

"It was raining that day, too," I said under my breath. "And pitch-black."

Ronny turned to me. "How do you know that?"

"I . . . it's in the poem," I said.

I didn't know if it was in the poem or not. But how do you say "I remember that day in 1864. It was the day I died"?

Uh-huh. Right.

"It's time," said Jem. He spun on his worn heels and hurried down the wooden stairs. I followed.

SIX

Train of Wagons

"Derek, I just got up here," Abby called after me as I started down the stairs.

"You can sure stay," I heard the guide say.

"Save it, Frodo," she said, and I almost smiled as I continued on my way, while Ronny hung back, scanning the ground below. "Derek, wait for me —"

But Jem had reached the bottom of the tower and retreated quickly into the trees. I couldn't wait. I hurried after him. Going down the stairs was easier than climbing up them, at least.

The young soldier took giant steps through the sludge of soggy ground, keeping on the edge of the woods until he paused near the old barn I'd seen from the tower.

As I trudged toward the barn, a wagon filled with reenactors rolled out of the woods onto the big field. Another one followed it, and more after that. I counted at least twenty wagons before I saw Jem slide into the dark barn through a side door. I glanced back. Abby and Ronny hustled through the rain and followed me inside.

The place smelled like rotten wood and vermin.

Jem headed to the dim back corner of the barn. Suddenly, the shadows shifted, and a half-dozen men stepped out next to Jem.

They were ghosts, too.

Every one of them was oddly familiar to me in some way — a pair of squinting eyes, a mustache, a cocked hat, grizzled cheeks, a limp, a pained grin. They all rippled vaguely through my brain.

The whole thing was insanity.

But when I saw those faces and remembered them, even just a little bit, I knew that something like a vault in my mind must have cracked. The train wreck had busted it open. Memories were oozing out. Lines of some old poem. Emotions. Knowledge. Facts. The ability to see and hear ghosts.

Terror.

Now that I was at the scene of Ulysses' greatest act, closing the Wound — and his death — everything was coming back to me in a flood.

"We have barns all over Shongaloo," said Ronny, glancing around in the dark. "But I hate this kind."

"What's wrong with it?" Abby asked, shivering.

"It's h-h-haunted," he said, turning away from the ghosts. Even though Ronny couldn't see them, he could tell where they were. He stared sullenly out the open barn door, watching the wagons pass. He was decaying on the outside — I could see the growing patch of gray flesh on his neck — but he was decaying inside, too. He couldn't see or hear the ghosts anymore. And now he stuttered.

I could see *and* hear the ghosts. Lucky me.

They tottered back and forth, every black eye on me.

"So the Grand Return is happening now? Today?" I asked. "Is that what's coming? More Legion soldiers? How can anyone stop it?"

"Wild horses galloped onto the Long Bridge," one ghost said. "Horses and men crashed off the side, into the water. You remember that. That's how I died."

"Some say K set up that ambush," a second put in.

"K?" I repeated. "Who's K?"

Ronny spun around. "What? Did you say K? Is K here?"

A tall, hatless ghost with one arm spoke next. "He's around. I saw him sneaking among the rocks at Cross Crag."

A new character? I wanted to hurl again. I clutched Ulysses' book and remembered a phrase from the poem.

. . . the nameless one . . .

I turned to Ronny. "They say K is here. Who is he?"

"He's . . . something different," Ronny said quietly.

"Evil?" asked Abby, quick to jump in. "Is K evil? Is he in the Legion?"

"I never found out," Ronny said, pacing through the barn door, in and out of the rain. "Maybe, maybe not. I met him once in the afterlife. I didn't like him. No one did. Maybe he wants to get rid of the First. Maybe he wants to get rid of others *for* the First. Who knows?" Ronny's eyes narrowed. "K learned to mask his sound in the afterlife, so we would n-n-ever even know if he was here. . . ."

"That boy's right," said Jem, his eyes shrinking. "K is trouble."

Ronny muttered under his breath and stepped fully into the rain. He hunched his shoulders, turning his head and trying to listen. He took a step away from the barn. Another step.

"Ronny, don't you dare leave us," said Abby.

"I r-r-remember him," Ronny stammered. "If he's on the battlefield, he could lead us to the First." He turned to face me. His drenched skin darkened by the moment. "I can't see ghosts anymore, I can't hear the First, but I can try to find K. Maybe he'll r-r-emember me. Maybe he'll show himself to me. I'm going out there."

"Ronny, no," said Abby, moving into the rain and grabbing his arm. "We shouldn't split up. Don't —"

But I knew Ronny would go.

"I g-g-gotta," he said. "It's the only thing I can think to do. Derek, read that b-book!" He stumbled down the wagon path, toward the outcropping called Cross Crag, and was gone.

Abby groaned softly, looking at me. I just stood there. Why didn't I rush after him?

I wanted him with me. I *needed* him with me. He was Ronny, my brother! Except that he wasn't, not really. He wasn't Ronny, and I wasn't Derek. Everything was falling apart, and he was just one of the pieces.

I didn't know what to do. I didn't know anything.

One of the ghosts broke into my thoughts. "You're the special one," he said. "You bleed. They say the First bled, too."

A short man with black hair added, "Only two of you bleeders so far."

That ran through my veins like ice. I was getting used to the feeling.

The ghost with the black hair rested his hand on the shoulder of a figure in a gray cap, who seemed to be kneeling on the hay. His head was only waist high.

"I fell with the First at Cerro Gordo," that ghost said. He shuffled forward awkwardly in the hay. I saw that he had only the top half of his legs.

I tried not to look.

"He was a colonel in the Mexican War in 1847," the legless ghost went on. "And a madman, and a savage. They call him the First because he was the first one who came back."

"Tell me about him," I said, moving closer to the ghosts. Abby followed, hearing only my side of the conversation.

"For fifteen years, the First rose in the ranks of the Legion in the afterlife," the soldier without legs told me. "Before him, the Legion was just a rabble of dead souls. But he pulled them together and led a big revolt against the good souls. Then the Wound tore open, and he escaped. Captain Ulysses discovered him. But when Ulysses closed the Wound, the First remained."

"He *remained*?" I said. "Here?"

I heard Abby gasp softly. "Who?"

"Fat Henry, tell the captain what happened to you," said Jem. He motioned to a tall, gaunt man — the opposite of fat — standing like a statue in the corner. The tall ghost stepped forward, pawing the side of his head again and again. It was like a nervous tic.

"I can never forget it," Fat Henry said in a soft voice. "He took my body for a while, used it up. He found another."

The man didn't focus on me. His eyes, dead black, looked like they were glistening with tears.

It didn't make sense. I shook my head. "How did he do it?"

"He took my body for a while, used it up. He found another. He took my body . . ."

"Derek, I hear a noise outside," said Abby, tugging on my sleeve. "Trucks, maybe. Do you hear them?"

I blinked, looked at her. "Yes . . . but . . ."

"It's them, isn't it?" she said. "The Legion. They're finally here."

I tried to understand. It wasn't working. Too much at once.

I turned back to Jem. "Are you saying the First came back during the Battle of Cemetery Bend, and he stayed? For over a hundred and forty years?"

"He took my body for a while . . . ," Fat Henry repeated.

"What's happening?" asked Abby.

"The ghosts are saying that the First stayed," I said. "He was trapped out of the Wound – on this side. He took over one body after another."

Her eyes narrowed, and her face clouded. "You mean he kept killing people? So he could inhabit a new body whenever he needed one? That's . . . horrible. But there would be proof, wouldn't there?"

"Seriously? Proof?" I shook my head. "There's an opening to the afterlife and dead guys are pouring through, and you want to be logical?"

"Don't snap at me! I'm your friend here. Your only friend, if you don't count your snooty brother, who couldn't wait to take off and look for S or W or whoever."

"K," I said.

"Whatever. My mother told me to stick with you. And maybe we'll never even see Ronny again."

The thought jarred me.

The ghosts drifted off. Jem stood just outside the barn doorway. Heavy rain poured through him.

"Now to where the phantom was born," he said.

"What?" I said. That word again.

"By the river, through the stones. It's in the book." With that, Jem walked into the rain.

What was that supposed to mean? Having a ghost guide was helpful, I guessed, but I couldn't help thinking that I would have liked Jem more if he wasn't so cryptic.

Clutching the cartridge box that hung from my shoulder, I turned to Abby. "Jem says I have to go —"

Without any further explanation, I walked straight out of the barn after the ghost. Abby followed. Rain drenched us all over again.

I didn't know what "through the stones" meant. I had no idea what I would find by the river, either. But I knew I had to go.

SEVEN

A Poem of the Long War

I couldn't see much in the pelting rain. It wasn't easy to follow a ghost in this mess.

We tramped along the edge of the woods to where it opened onto Bloody Meadow. I pressed the cartridge box tightly to my side, knowing that the book was safe inside. Abby scrambled along behind me.

Jem stumbled toward the river, muttering to himself about the book. It was all in the book.

I'd read only snatches of it so far. I hadn't exactly had quiet time for story hour. But I knew I would have to read the whole poem before the day was over if I was ever going to figure this out. For now, I'd just have to rely on what I could remember. The pouring rain wasn't the best place to pull out an old book, but I'll tell you what I know.

The Ghost Road: A Poem of the Long War was more than a thousand lines long. The fine black-ink handwriting that began the poem soon gave way to more of a quick scrawl. By the end, the writing was frantic — sometimes illegible.

The poem was divided into four parts, which he wrote over three years until his death. Across the first page were faint block letters, slightly slanted: *Amaranthia — 1861.* An inch or so down from that heading, Ulysses began his poem.

Within your crimson walls, I was an angel child;
From room to room I floated in your wingless window light . . .

He went on about his childhood, which was happy and sunlit. I'd already memorized those words.

O Amaranthia,
When on your blossoming fields I played young captain,
With my boyhood mate, young Thomas Bell —

Riding our ponies breakneck o'er the hills,
Or playing boats and underboats along the riverbank
(His dubbed the Crux, *mine* Spectre *was) —*

We were immortal sons of your Elysium,
But little knew what lay ahead for us — what lay ahead!

There was more, about his family, his days in school as he and Tom Bell grew up, college in the North, his sweetheart, and then the day that he and Tom rode off to war.

I'd read enough Civil War history to know that both sides, the Union and the Confederacy, predicted that victory would be theirs easily. Except that there was no victory. Not for either side. Fighting dragged on through four long years.

I wiped the water from my face.

I had to duck off the path when a troop of reenactors burst noisily out of the woods and onto the field. Abby darted after me. But Jem kept striding away. The reenactors couldn't see him. The troop hustled along the edge of the woods until they reached a stone wall. They followed it to a break, slipped behind it, and went on their way.

"Derek," said Abby, "this is weirding me out. Can you please say something? Don't pull a Ronny on me, okay? Where are we going? Are we lost?"

I turned to look after Jem and spotted something through the trees. A few plaques had been set up, by battlefield restoration groups, I guessed.

"We're not lost," I said.

Beyond the trees was a thin, flat stone, cracked and leaning. There were other stones all around, some upright, some flat on the ground. Rain scoured the words on their mottled faces.

Now I knew what "through the stones" meant.

"The cemetery."

EIGHT

Dead Boy Walking

Pushing through the overgrown shrubs and vines, I saw rows of marble markers snaking into the distance, one after another down to the water. Jem made his way slowly across the cemetery.

He was talking to the stones.

A low growl in my bad ear told me that Erskine Cane was getting closer. Waldo Fouks, too. And behind them both was that constant rumbling — lower than the deepest human voices — of the gathering Legion.

They were almost at the battlefield.

"There must be thousands of graves here," Abby said quietly, looking around.

It was true. Jem peered down at one stone, then collapsed to his knees, the rain still washing through him. From where I stood, I could read the name etched on the stone — Frederick Ross. Jem's brother?

"He died in a ditch," Jem said over his shoulder. "They all died in ditches."

Old Tom and I, unhorsed, retreated to the meadow,
Its deep-gouged earth, all ditches, channeled by the rain . . .

"Derek?" said Abby. She could tell that something was going on with me.

My skull ached from the flood of memories, the poem. I felt attacked. Ulysses was always there, talking in my head. I hated it. I hated him. If I didn't hate him, he would take over, wouldn't he?

And if he took over . . . who would I be?

Abby broke into my thoughts again. "Derek, will you please talk to me?"

So I talked.

Even though I tried to hold them back, the words spilled out. I told her how Union soldiers descended on Ulysses and his friend Tom during the battle. They flew out of the woods, across the sodden ditches of the meadow.

"Ulysses drew his cavalry saber," I said. "It belonged to his grandfather. A Union soldier knocked him back with his rifle. The saber broke when he fell. Three Federals jumped at him, but Tom Bell grabbed the broken saber and thrust himself between the soldiers and his friend."

Abby watched me closely. "This is in the poem?"

"Yes," I said. It was, but it was also burned into my memory somewhere. I knew that now. "And then, somehow, the saber — Ulysses' broken saber — flew up. Tom Bell screamed. The saber cut deep."

Abby turned pale. "Gross."

"It was," I said, seeing the scene in front of me. "Tom fell into a ditch and went still. Ulysses watched the ditch water bubble and splash over his face."

Abby shook her head slowly. I went on.

"After that, another bunch of Union soldiers charged out from the woods, and Ulysses ducked behind the wall over there to hide. I remem — Ulysses wrote about those cold minutes, waiting for the troops to move off. When they finally left, he searched the bodies lying in the field. He stumbled over the flooded ground until he heard a sudden splash and saw a man lurch up —"

Though it was getting weirder by the minute, I remembered the scene and the words at the same time.

Tom grasped my arm, ferocious as some maddened
animal,
Bellowing, "I live! I live! I live!"

And that was it. What Ulysses saw in that moment was the first translation. My knees wobbled with the realization.

Was that really the way it had happened? Had Thomas Bell become the First? Was it his best friend?

He whirled my broken saber in the air and sheathed it
on his side.
"A keepsake, if I may," he said, "of having died."
"You are welcome to it, my friend," I said to him.

My racing mind was interrupted by the sound of sobbing. Jem's face was in his hands as he quaked at his brother's grave. His tears mingled with the rain.

I knew how he felt.

I remembered feeling the same way at Ronny's empty tomb in New Orleans. Only . . . it *wasn't* my brother's tomb, was it? Ronny was Virgil Black by then, and I was already Ulysses Longtemps. We weren't brothers at all.

We were nothing, only I hadn't known it yet.

I turned to Abby. I had put it off for too long. I had to tell her. I had to get it out of me. It was like throwing up all over again.

"Abby . . . that happened to me, too."

She stepped back, pushing her hair out of her face. "What? You know someone who died like Tom, then came back? You mean Ronny?"

"No. Me." I could barely look at her.

"What?"

A light from the dredger flashed across the cemetery. Jem bolted to his feet. He stumbled away through the gravestones like a frightened deer and plunged into the woods toward the riverbank. "Come on," he called. "No time!"

Groaning voices sounded from the road behind us. "Hurry," I said to Abby. We'd have to finish our conversation later. It was just as well.

I hustled after Jem from one crooked path to another. We ran for what felt like half an hour before we wound up on the rutted streets at the outskirts of Cemetery Bend. The village was a nothing of a place. But once I stepped through the fog and onto those streets, it felt like I had walked the route a hundred times.

"Derek!" Abby's call came from far back. The girl was recovering from a fractured ankle, after all. "Where are we going?"

I slowed. "A building by the river. Jem says it's where the phantom was born."

I couldn't see her face clearly from this far away, but I was pretty sure she rolled her eyes. "Oh, great. What does that even mean?" she said.

I didn't answer, just waited for her to catch up and followed Jem down a crooked street. Most of it wasn't paved. Brick buildings lined the street on one side, and the river was on the other.

I thought I heard a splash, turned, and saw something moving beneath the water just beyond the street. What was it? A shape? A face?

Whatever it was, it was keeping pace with me.

A voice spoke: *We are ready!*

I tried to keep a grip on my sanity. Easier said than done. Abby didn't see the shape. Didn't hear it speak. Of course she didn't.

I had to tell her about me. Then she'd understand. "Abby, something happened to me —"

"Look," she interrupted, staring past me to the end of the street.

A solitary black building loomed — half piled up the riverbank, half falling into the water.

We were there.

NINE

The Manufactory

"What is it?" Abby asked. "Some kind of factory?"

Jem hovered in the shadows of the building.

"Manufactory," I said. It was a word I'd never said out loud before. "Well, yeah. It's a factory."

It was a low, thick, brick-faced structure built down a slope from the road. One story fronted the road, but there were two on the waterside.

Abby started walking toward the building. "What's inside?"

"I don't know," I said, falling into step with her.

But didn't I?

I tugged the Ulysses book out of the cartridge case. I flipped the pages, past the part where Ulysses left home to fight.

The second section was called *The Manufactory 1862–1863* and was scratched in several different-colored inks. The pages were greasy, creased with dirt. Just scanning them, I knew that the poem focused on Ulysses becoming a cavalry officer, and followed him through the first two years of fighting.

I tried to be all things — poet, thinker, husband, officer,
Surgeon, friend. But like my men, these died off one by one
Until everything I was . . . was just a soldier.

I wondered what Ronny might have been if he hadn't become "just a soldier," fighting the dead in the afterlife. Was that what I was supposed to be, too?

Further on, I read how something had happened to change Ulysses.

Then came a light into my darkness. A memory and vision
Of some one thing to end this war and drive it from our land.
Thus boy-I-was and man-I-am combined. And I began my work.

I've already told you that I didn't like poetry. It was, of course, kind of a sick joke that Ulysses had turned out to be a poet, because I'd always hated the stuff so much. But were lines like these the "code" my mother had told me I had to decipher?

What did the guy mean — *boy-I-was and man-I-am combined*?

Ugh.

"Derek?" said Abby. "I see a light inside."

I glanced up, but turned back to the pages.

"Listen to this." I read aloud as we walked.

"'I chose a secret building by the shore — my manufactory.

And kept a vigil lonely and alone. Me and my phantom.'"

"Okay, but who's the phantom?" Abby asked.

I didn't know, and said so, though the word meant something to me. Reading that scrawled word on the yellowed page, I felt like I was dropping quickly through water.

"Are we going in or not?" Abby rubbed her arms. "It's cold out here."

There was a reason for that — besides the rain. Jem was standing behind Abby's shoulder, shaking his head. "She sticks with you, doesn't she?"

I pulled Abby away from him and approached the river side of the building. Jem walked past and vanished through the wall.

The bricks were uneven. The mortar had long ago cracked and spilled out between them. The roof tiles were slate, mostly chipped, a few missing. The place looked long-abandoned — except for that single dull glow against the high windows. It cast a dirty yellow sheen onto the pavement.

"How do we even get into this place?" Abby asked. "The door has no handle on it."

I tried *not* to remember, but I couldn't help myself.

"Stand back. Please."

Reaching over our heads, I pressed my fingers against the doorframe and moved them slowly along the rough red mortar. I found what I was looking for and pulled. An iron lever shifted. The door popped open an inch or two.

Abby whistled. "Well, look at you, the expert in old buildings. . . ."

All at once, the door swung wide, and the barrel of a gun was pressed against my forehead.

"Hands up! Or I'll shoot you where you stand!"

TEN

By a Candle's Flame

I put my hands up. Abby slipped into the shadows.

Smart girl.

"That's right, son. Keep them high. I might be little, but from this range, my pistol won't miss!"

The woman beyond the door *was* little, but she kept the pistol pressed firmly against my head. She was about my mother's age and wore thick glasses and a slouchy beret.

"That will probably misfire," I said, surprising myself.

The woman blinked. "Excuse me? What was that?"

Yeah, what *was* that? I can't tell you how, but I recognized the gun. Unlike the replicas the reenactors used, this one was real. But the pistol happened to have a problem that I knew about. Somehow.

"That's a Colt Navy revolver," I said. "Damp air makes them jam."

The woman looked at the gun in her hand. "It does?"

I nodded. "That was the joke about them. It's a Navy revolver that doesn't work when it's wet."

"Now, that's just weird, Derek," Abby said, coming into the light of the open door. "How would you know that?"

When the woman saw Abby, she jerked the pistol at her but finally lowered and uncocked it. "Hmpf. I guess most thieves don't bring their girlfriends with them —"

"Girlfriends?" Abby snorted. "There are no girlfriends here!"

She said it as if it were a bad word. But there were bigger things than my ego to deal with now.

"You're a spicy thing, aren't you?" the woman said. "This place is off-limits to those beer-bellied reenactors. Don't want them pawing at my work. But you kids come along in, out of the rain. Though it's not so funny, me holding a gun on you. I've been attacked twice — once at home, once in my hotel. Fire at the hotel that time." She turned and disappeared inside, leaving the door open behind her.

A fire? Abby and I looked at each other. I knew we were thinking the same thing —Erskine Cane, the arsonist. Why would he go after *her*?

But when I saw the long room of the workshop inside, I got my answer. I knew it. I had spent many hours in that very room.

Nightly in that long room, my courage drained,
Guttering like a failing candle flame . . .

My knees buckled under me.

"Whoa, you okay?" the woman asked.

"He's just a little wobbly," said Abby, holding me up.

"On account of?"

"On account of Derek sees ghosts," Abby said matter-of-factly.

"Ghosts?" The woman blinked again, then laughed heartily. "I see ghosts all the time!" She laid the revolver down on a workbench. "My name is Mercedes Bloom. Professor Bloom to my students. I teach Civil War history at Tulane in New Orleans. History is full of ghosts."

Yeah, not quite the same. Little did she know that a ghost was sitting at her desk that very moment. I glanced at Jem, then back at Professor Bloom.

"How did you find my secret place?" she asked.

"Yeah, Derek," said Abby, "how *did* you find this place?"

My eyes were drawn to the shadows at the far end of the room. My heart thudded, then skipped.

And yet I pressed myself with keenest eye and agile hand,
To craft a lung of iron, an iron crypt, whose breath was merest silence.

I knew then what stood in the shadows.

"The *Phantom* is a submarine," I said aloud.

"So! You've heard of my work!" Smiling cautiously, Professor Bloom pulled a lever on the wall. A large tubular object was instantly bathed in spotlight.

Abby drew in a breath. "Holy submarine, Batman."

Fifteen feet from nose to tail, the *Phantom* looked like a giant iron cigar. Fins jutted out along the sides. A cone on top was chopped flat like a hat.

The hull was made of plates rounded and fastened by big rivets and thick gobs of hasty welding. There was a porthole the size of a pie plate on the brow of the rounded nose. It looked like a glass eye. A propeller pointed downward at an angle from the rear.

"This is a replica of an old submarine called the *Phantom*," said Professor Bloom. "It was built in 1864 —"

"By Ulysses Longtemps," I cut in. I couldn't stop shaking.

Professor Bloom's eyebrows shot up. "How do you know that name?"

"I'm . . . a Longtemps," I said.

Little did she know.

Professor Bloom whistled quietly. "A Longtemps! Then you'll know that even though Ulysses was a captain in the Louisiana cavalry, he was also a wealthy engineer. Something happened, I don't know exactly what, but he designed and built the *Phantom* on his own time to help the war effort. Took him two years. It was only used once. And Longtemps died on its maiden voyage, drowned after it exploded underwater."

Part of me trembled to hear all that from a stranger.

My fingers tingled as I reached out to touch the iron. I traced the head of each rivet, cupped my hands around the porthole frame, and peeked inside. The replica was amazingly close to the submarine lodged in my memory — the one I hadn't even remembered at all until a minute before.

"Up until last year, we thought there was nothing left of the sub but these plans," said Professor Bloom, gesturing to blueprints spread out over her workbench. "Then I actually found part of the submarine about two miles downriver of here." She pointed to a chart of the Red River tacked to the wall.

I shook even more.

Two miles? Was that where the Wound was?

"I started researching the *Eastport* disaster, then discovered a rusted metal fin that matched the plans," she said. "It had fused somehow with the bedrock of the river, as if by incredible heat. Impossible to retrieve. Luckily I took its measurements. With all the dredging, it's impossible to know if it's still there."

"Uh-huh," I said, moving around the submarine, trying to listen to what she was saying. I hoped Abby was paying attention. My mind was falling backward in time. I imagined Ulysses hammering rivets, welding seams, setting the delicate instruments into the submarine's nose.

"The *Phantom* was revolutionary in several ways," the professor said, happy to have an audience. It reminded me of that moment on the train before the crash, when Dad described his love of trains.

A long time ago.

"The pneumatic bladders were invented in 1845," I said, blurting out some crazy words. Where had they come from? "Ulysses used them for buoyancy. The crew could either pump in air or pump out water."

Professor Bloom made a face. "You doing a report on your great-grandfather's old sub or something?"

"Or something," I said.

Spotting a computer on a small desk nearby, Abby gasped. "Oh my gosh, can I go online?" She barely waited for Professor Bloom's answer before sliding into a chair at the worktable and plugging her phone into an empty charger.

The professor shrugged. "Knock yourself out."

I knew what Abby was looking for — something to verify that the First had stayed behind after

Ulysses had closed the Wound. I already believed he had — but Abby needed more. Discovering a pattern of odd deaths around Cemetery Bend over the last century and a half might be the way to convince her — and others.

I couldn't take my hands off the submarine, as if I thought it would give me answers. But when I noticed a small plastic propeller on the back, beneath the larger, copper one, I stopped cold. "This isn't right."

"There's a small engine," Professor Bloom explained. "I want to pilot the sub underwater, but the university won't let me take it out unless there's a backup engine. All the old subs sank, you know. The engine doesn't compromise the integrity of the design, just adds a safety backup." She hooted a laugh. "Never mind that there's only about a half hour of usable air in one of these things, anyway!"

"Is it sea-proof?" asked Abby, listening from the computer terminal.

"Seaworthy," I said.

"It doesn't need to be," I heard Jem whisper. "Not all that long, anyway." He was slumped on the floor now, with his eyes closed.

Professor Bloom smiled. "I've lowered her into the water, and she doesn't leak. After the dredger moves downriver, I'll take her out."

Abby clicked away on the computer, murmuring. "Oh man, oh man."

The clock on the wall chimed two. The high windows showed that the sky was even darker than before. Time was passing, but it felt like we were standing still.

Not the Legion, though. Their voices had been circling louder and louder since we'd heard the trucks when we were in the barn. What were they waiting for? How long before they would move across the fields, the woods, the swamps, the riverbank?

And what about Ronny? Was he finding anything out about this K person? How long had it been since he'd run off? Was he safe?

Too many questions.

"Do you want to sit inside?" Professor Bloom asked, popping open the *Phantom*'s top latch. "You can, if you like."

Abby looked over at the submarine. Jem did, too.

"I . . . thanks," I said. My hands shook as I climbed a short ladder and lowered myself into the top hatch. I slid inside the sub without difficulty. Was I getting thinner? Maybe all that running was paying off after all.

My breath quickened the second I sat on the cold iron seat. My throat constricted. I felt something brush my shoulder, then a movement next to me. I looked around the unlit submarine. Nothing.

Then another touch. Cold fingers on my arm. I turned again, quaking from head to toe.

A pale young face stared at me in the dark. The face had the faint shadow of a beard. Its owner was a few years older than Ronny, about the same age as Ulysses in the photo I'd seen. He had long brown hair, but his features weren't young and vibrant. He looked ghostly and gray with pain, aged before his time.

I'd known him forever.

"Tom . . . ?"

Abby called out from the computer. "Derek? You okay in there?"

"Tom," I whispered. He nodded once to me.

It was Thomas Bell, Ulysses' best friend. Old Tom. Every bit of their childhood together came rushing back to me. Playing by the riverbank, riding horses at Amaranthia. Then Tom's death in the ditch on Bloody Meadow, and the moment when he stood up and said, "I live!"

Now I wasn't just remembering what I'd read in the poem. These were my memories. Ulysses' memories.

I was momentarily afraid when Tom's face

appeared, but I knew immediately that the First wasn't inside him anymore.

"Tom," I whispered, "what happened in the submarine? The poem's unfinished. What really happened at the end —"

Old Tom seemed to breathe hard, without using any breath at all. Then he pawed the side of his head as Fat Henry had. I remembered then that they both had been killed the same way: in a flooded ditch with Ulysses' broken saber buried in the sides of their heads.

I heard a far-off noise outside the sub, outside the building. Someone was calling out. I couldn't hear what the voice was saying.

Tom stumbled over words, barely audible, and I had to move even closer. The air around him was frigid. I had never been so close to a ghost before. And now here we were, cramped inside this metal coffin, face-to-face.

"Blood . . . ," I thought he said.

"What?"

The faraway voice echoed in my ear again.

As I watched Tom, I felt like retching, or weeping, or drowning, or something. I kept remembering the broken saber, the wound on his head, the ditch.

He spoke up finally. "My . . . blood . . ."

All at once, Old Tom's face turned as pale as snow.

He clamped a hand over his sliced ear, then faded into nothing — but not before reaching out and touching my hand.

I gasped for air. I found none. I was drowning all over again, in no water this time. I reached for the hatch but fumbled it, and it slammed down over me, plunging me into darkness. I banged on the hull, screaming. I couldn't breathe.

Suddenly, the hatch popped up and Abby was there, dragging me out by my wrists. I collapsed to the floor. Professor Bloom had the phone to her ear. "Emergency —"

"No! Hang up, please!" Abby cried. "He has fits. It's okay. I know what to do. Hang up, please. Maybe some water?"

The professor hung up the phone and hustled off to another room to get a glass of water.

Abby leaned over me. "Are you going to make it?" Jem hovered in the shadows, watching.

"I'm okay. . . ." But I wasn't.

I realized now that the voice in my ear, so faint and far away, was Ronny's. He was calling out, crying, in trouble. And I heard him.

"Then listen," Abby whispered. "I think I found it. In 1927, 1960, and 1982. There were more, I bet, but I could only find those three. When the police discovered a body, someone went missing. When that person turned up dead, another person vanished. Derek, the First *did* survive —"

Glass exploded across the room. A smoking bottle flew through the broken window onto the floor and shattered. Jem vanished instantly.

Professor Bloom screamed. "Now we call 911!"

The door thudded and began to splinter. Abby grabbed her phone from the charger and dialed while the professor heaved her desk against the door.

"Leave me alone!" Professor Bloom cried out. "What do you people want?"

The room was so thickly lined with iron that it muffled the voices from outside. Was Cane out there? I couldn't tell, but I couldn't hang around to find out.

I heard Ronny's voice in my ear again.

"We need to get out of here!" I said, turning to the professor.

"I have to protect the sub!" said Professor Bloom. She tapped a code into a keypad on the wall. The submarine lowered into a tank beneath the factory, directly into the river. A thick iron plate sealed the top of the tank.

"You can only get to it from underneath," the professor said. "It'll be safe." She stuffed her own cell into her pocketbook, slung the bag over her shoulder, and ran for a circular staircase. "Up to the parking lot. My car —"

More glass shattered.

We bolted up the curving stairs and out a side door into an alley at the street level. Abby moved as quickly as she could on her still-healing ankle. We ran breathlessly, toppling over garbage cans. I heard a jangle of keys, and Professor Bloom grabbed us by the arms. "Both of you — inside!"

We all dived into her Jeep and roared away, not seeing who had attacked the factory. But Abby and I knew. The Legion was everywhere. Sirens already worked their way through the streets.

"To the battlefield," I said, trying to catch my breath. "My brother . . . needs help."

"I'm not even going to ask how you know that," Professor Bloom said, jerking the steering wheel. "Just fasten your seat belts!"

ELEVEN

The Cemetery at the Bend

The battlefield wasn't that far away, but Professor Bloom had to follow the winding streets. Well, some of them. She raced the Jeep within an inch of its life, slicing corners, bounding onto sidewalks, skidding across lanes — just like Ronny would have.

"The more I think about this," the professor said, gunning through a red light, "the more I think you kids ought to be in school."

"It's summer," said Abby.

"Summer school, then," the professor said. "I'm getting out of here and going back to New Orleans. No way is grading papers as dangerous as this!"

She didn't know the half of it. I hoped she wouldn't have to.

The Legion's voices ground constantly in my ear now, sometimes loud, sometimes soft. But they never disappeared. The Legion was spreading across the battlefield, and I still didn't know exactly what they planned to do, or where to find the First.

Or what to do when I found him.

Ronny's voice was louder and closer . . . and he was in pain.

"Stop before you get to the police cordon," I said as Professor Bloom tore through the puddles flooding Swamp Road.

The Jeep splashed into a rut and splashed back out again. "End of the line," said the professor, sliding to a muddy stop a few hundred yards from the battlefield. "You want me to stay?"

"No," I said, scrambling out of the Jeep and closing the door behind me. "You should get as far away as possible."

The moment the professor roared off, Abby and I ran through the woods and past the tower, not stopping until we reached the cemetery fence. We heard groaning and branches cracking.

"Ronny?" I called.

There was a flash of light from among the tombstones, then the sound of hooves fading into the distance. By the time we got to Ronny, he was alone. He sank into the rain-softened ground on one knee. His left arm dangled, limp, by his side. A smell hung in the air, but it wasn't Ronny's smell of decay. It was different. A chemical odor, it smelled odd, thick, sharp, and disgusting — even in the rain.

"Who was it?" I asked, kneeling next to him.

He turned his face to me. One pupil was large and wild, the other as tiny as the head of a pin. His shirt was cut to ribbons at his shoulder. I saw slice marks on his skin, but not a trace of blood. There never was with Ronny.

Abby and I helped him to his feet. He leaned against a tree trunk.

"K is on the field somewhere. The s-s-spy. I w-was following him," he said. "He lured me here. I think it was a trap. You never know with K. But K wasn't here when I arrived. The other was here instead."

"Can you move your arm?" asked Abby, scanning him for other injuries.

"The other was here instead," he repeated. "He came at me from behind. I think there were ghosts here. I didn't see them." He turned to me. "Your g-g-ghosts, Derek."

My ghosts? Had he guessed that I was Ulysses? Did he know what my mother had told me? Or was he just thinking of Jem and the others?

Ronny shot a glance to the left, and I followed it with my eyes. Three or four ghosts lingered in the darkness under the pines. They were the ghosts from the barn. Ronny's eyes darted back and forth, but he still didn't see them.

"I th-think the ghosts spoke, but they couldn't do

anything," he went on. "The darkness was too heavy for them."

"The darkness?" Abby repeated. "Ronny, who fought you?"

But I already knew.

Feeling a weight of darkness wash over me,

I took Tom's shoulders in my hands . . .

Ronny's cheek darkened as he spoke. "I could b-barely touch him. My fingers screamed to f-f-fight him off. Derek, it was him. The F-f-first. Evil."

I shuddered. "You saw his face?" In my mind I saw a mass of gray, mottled skin. But it merged with the face of Tom Bell. I tried to focus. "Ronny, you saw him?"

He shook his head, grimacing. "I c-couldn't l-l-look."

Ronny's neck was almost completely black now. He caught me glancing at it.

"Am I t-talking right?" he said suddenly.

"No," said Abby. "You need to rest —"

"The Legion came for us at the factory," I said, changing the subject. "Ulysses built a submarine. The *Phantom*. There's a replica —"

"So what?" Ronny snapped, pushing both of us away and standing on his own. "A toy boat? There are k-killers on the field!"

"I think it means something about the Wound," I said.

We heard engines roaring and shots – real shots – and grunting and the splashing of men falling in water. The first sounds of attack. The Legion had started to push reenactors toward the river.

"The battle has s-s-started," said Ronny.

Troops of soldiers were moving into position, exactly as they had in 1864. The massacre in the flooded field, the ambush on the bridge – all the forces were riding and running to where they needed to be.

The pinging of real musket fire in the trees came then, followed by wild yelling. A brigade of reenactors ran out of the woods into the cemetery.

"Get out of here!" I yelled at them.

"Who are you guys?" one middle-aged man with glasses cried, throwing a look of terror over his shoulder. They all ran faster.

I dragged Ronny to the ground and pulled Abby with us.

Smoke swirled as thick as clay around the men, washing out from the trees behind them like waves of fog.

"Retreat?" yelled one. "But the directions say we advance two miles –"

Were some of the fake soldiers still playing?

Didn't they know?

"Get out of here!" I yelled, standing. "The attackers are real!"

And there they were.

The translated dead stumbled out from the trees. I recognized tourists from the bayou, townspeople from New Compson. Their dark shapes moved relentlessly, ragged but determined and swift. Some had rifles. Others had swords, and they used them.

I saw Santa, the bearded man from the campfire. His face was no more than a tangled gray beard, his mouth screaming a big dark O of panic. His yell joined with other noises in the confusion — running footfalls, crying, laughing, bursts of musket fire, momentary silence, and a storm of howls. A mass of fake soldiers ran like madmen right at us.

They rushed among the gravestones, leaping over and around them. I had to step aside, was pushed down, tried to get up, was pushed away. "No —"

Ronny cried, "Derek, get back here! Abby!"

I reached for Abby's arm. But she was torn away from me in the rush of bodies.

"Abby!" I cried. "Abby!" I called over and over, stumbling toward where I'd last seen her. Waves of men rushed past me, knocked me down again. I struggled to get up. There was a crash in the trees to my left. My bad ear rang uncontrollably. I could barely hear anything but the ringing.

I bolted in the direction the men had gone.

"Ronny!" I called out. "Abby —"

A horse galloped through the trees. Five horses. Ten. A cavalry troop overran the cemetery. I dashed aside and was suddenly alone in the dark.

"Abby! Ronny!"

I couldn't hear them. Above the ringing in my ear I heard the sound of musket fire in the distance and the thundering of hooves approaching again.

I ran.

TWELVE

Dead Quiet

Dark shapes moved in the woods on both sides of the cemetery. Men — living men — rushed among the gravestones and into the flooded ditches beyond. Some yelled, most ran, some even laughed, having no idea that their attackers were real or that their comrades were actually dying.

Water splashed over and over. The whole battlefield was soaked. Water was everywhere.

The translations had begun.

A troop of horsemen appeared on the far edge of the woods. These weren't weekend soldiers playing pretend. They wore the ashen faces of the dead.

"No, no, no . . ."

I spotted a rambling building on the edge of the cemetery. The stable I'd seen from the tower? Maybe Abby and Ronny had seen it, too. Holding the cartridge box tight under my arm, I ran, slogged low beside a stone wall, then lurched through the open field to the stable. I kicked open the door as if it were paper, and dived in before the dead saw me.

My brain was a mess. I needed time.

The stable had been converted into some kind of battlefield museum. Instead of housing horses, it was a house of war. And it was dead quiet.

No Ronny. No Abby.

Closed because of the reenactment, the rooms were nearly as dark as caves, with only grimy windows shedding a sick gray light. When my eyes adjusted to the dark, I made out display cases of documents, uniforms, weapons. I tugged at them. All locked. Bayonets and sabers stood in cases along the wall. Single-shot derringers and revolvers like Professor Bloom's were in a long set of cases, which ran the length of one side of the stable.

Outside, the cemetery was alive with shouts, grunts, thundering footsteps.

No, "alive" wasn't the right word. Not everyone making those noises was alive.

I peered around the stable, trying to distract myself, to gather my thoughts. On a pedestal beneath a gray window stood a tin model of the *Eastport*. What had Ronny called the *Phantom*? A toy? But it was more than that. If the explosion of the *Eastport* had caused the first Wound, had the *Phantom* somehow closed it?

I popped open Ulysses' cartridge box, pulled out the book, and pawed through the brittle pages. I flipped past the incident in the ditch. Past the First's translation into Tom. I wanted to read about the submarine.

Tom warns me of a thing he knows. That scuttled wreck,
The Eastport, *harbors secrets that will turn the war against us.*
His talk is veiled, he speaks in riddles, yet convinces me
Of a mission two or three might undertake in secrecy:
To blast that sunken ship to kingdom come.

Tom had already been taken over by the First, and he wanted to go to the site of the explosion. Why? To make the hole bigger? To bring more of the Legion here? When did Ulysses realize this? When did he truly understand about the Wound?

Thus Tom and I, and he, the nameless one, enter the deep.
The Phantom *takes me into it, that lung of iron,*
Its nose and tail with many charges filled.

"The nameless one?" I said aloud. Weirdly, I was comforted by the sound of my own voice. At least Ulysses hadn't taken over that. "K? Was K on the *Phantom* with Ulysses and Tom Bell?"

I turned to the end of the poem and found these lines on a page by themselves:

Confusion reigns as we approach the gaping Wound;

I steer and steer and steer and

Then nothing. *The Ghost Road* ended like that, in mid-line. How in the world was I supposed to —

A barrage of musket fire rattled in my good ear. Some shots sounded like hollow popping. Others were deeper, sharper — real shots.

I felt like crying. An insane, impossible war between the living and the dead was raging out there — and I was supposed to stop it!

With an unfinished poem?

With some ridiculous code?

Horses thundered past the stable. Horrified cries. The clang of steel.

I glanced at a saber in one display case. It wasn't for me. I picked up a chair and brought it down hard on the next case over. Glass flew everywhere. I grabbed a short folding dagger with a thick, almost tool-like blade. Don't ask me why. It seemed useful. I slipped it into my pocket just as a troop of mounted soldiers galloped by the busted stable door. I couldn't tell if they were living or dead, but I wasn't taking any chances. I ducked under the case, dragged it across the room after me, and used it to brace the door shut.

Chaos raged around the stable. I was being pulled back to the battle, and I was losing Derek Stone.

"But I *am* Derek," I said to the gray air. My voice was weak, pathetic. It sounded like I didn't even believe my own words.

I tried to remember what it was like to be me. The boy who'd started this story. The boy who lived in New Orleans.

"Derek, Derek, Derek," I whispered.

Breathing deeply, trying to calm down, I traced my finger across a framed map hanging on the wall nearby. I moved it from Alexandria to Bordelon — the train route — then from New Orleans to Bayou Malpierre to Baton Rouge to Coushatta to Cemetery Bend.

Would I ever be home in New Orleans again? It had been only a few days since I'd been there. But when you leave home, it always feels like forever since you've been there. You know what I mean.

My house on Royal Street was nothing but a burned-out shell now — Erskine Cane had seen to that. Uncle Carl was probably in a hotel somewhere, trying desperately to find me and Ronny. Big Bob Lemon, who'd helped me understand this insanity in the first place, was probably dead, though I didn't know for sure. And my father — what about him? I didn't even know.

No, there was nothing in New Orleans for me. I

doubted I'd ever see it again. It wasn't home anymore. Home was where Ronny and Abby were. But maybe even that would end today.

By end of day, I knew that dead love might be me.

An outburst of angry cries snapped me out of it again. I peeked through one of the windows. A troop of pretend Federals rushed past the cemetery's far wall toward the meadow. I'd wait for them to leave, then try to find Abby and Ronny. But what would we do? Where would we go? The First was out there. Time was running out.

None of the pieces were fitting together.

I noticed then that the wall map seemed to waver. The edges were tinged with red light. Was I losing my mind? That question almost made me laugh. But then there was an outline of a human shape on the map. The shape wobbled and grew larger as I stumbled backward.

"What —"

I felt the heat. The door behind me was on fire. Red flames licked up both sides of the doorframe and across the top, where they spread to the ceiling.

What I'd seen on the frame was a reflection.

Erskine Cane had found me.

The closest window burst into the room, spraying chunks of old glass and shards of wood across the floor. I shielded my eyes, but some glass caught me on the cheek and chin. I ran my hand across my face. I was bleeding.

"Throw me the book," Cane said, his face staring at me through the busted window.

A second wall was on fire, crackling with flame.

"Throw me the book!"

THIRTEEN

Cross Crag

Smoke thickened in the room. I ran to the far end, found a sliding door, and kicked the latch, snapping it. Pushing the door aside, I entered the unconverted stables. There were three stalls — not big, but not on fire. They had that going for them, anyway.

"Throw me the book!"

I could hear Cane, but I didn't know where he was. I held the cartridge box even tighter.

The whine of voices sounded all around the building. It was a tinderbox. Air burned in my lungs. Smoke filled my nostrils. I started to cough and thought I'd never stop. Above the roar of flames I heard horses whinnying outside.

And then . . . a shape moved inside the stable.

"Get away from me!" I shouted. The shape stopped. Cane's voice was still farther away, echoing distantly in my ears. This wasn't him.

Was it K? Ronny had said he could disguise his sound so no one could find him.

I moved away from the shape. "Get away —"

"Keep down!" a voice shouted over the roar of flames.

The wall next to me exploded with gunshot. I dived to the floor. It smelled like earth and rats and hay. More shots.

The shape reached me, shook me, its voice whispering gruffly in my ear. "Derek!"

I tried to focus. "Ronny?" I said. No, that wasn't right. No smell.

Suddenly, I was lifted powerfully to my feet. My knees buckled, and I fell back down.

"Derek, it's me."

Wiping the blood from my forehead, I made out the face. Deep eyes. Grizzled chin. I looked down to see a thickly bandaged hand. It couldn't be.

"Dad?"

"Derek, get up! You're out of time!"

I struggled to my feet. Even in the light of the flames, my father looked like death.

"There's an outcropping of rocks outside," he said.

Cross Crag. I knew it. "Okay . . ."

"I saw the girl run to them."

"Abby?" I asked. "Is she —"

"We have to get to the rocks," Dad said. He took my arm in his good hand and tugged it to keep me crouched down. "Be smart now. Stay low."

He pulled me to the only wall that wasn't burning . . . and kept going. Boards splintered when his shoulder struck it. Planks fell. What was that? How had he become so strong?

"There!" Cane's voice roared. Waldo was close, too. And the one-armed conductor from the train crash was running toward us. I saw them, heard them all.

My dad and I fell to the mud and struggled up, slipping and sliding, stumbling toward the river. We kept the burning museum between us and Cane. The field was broken by a group of huge glacial boulders, clustered, with winding paths between. This was Cross Crag. Rain hammered the rocks as we dashed among them.

"Abby!" I called.

"Shhhh!" Dad snapped.

"You said she was here —"

"Quiet," he said, searching ahead, looking for the way between the stones. "Stay here." He darted off, crouching. A moment later, he was back and motioned to me. My knuckles scraped against the rocks as I ran to catch up. He pulled me farther among the boulders and then collapsed against one, its blackness glistening in the rain.

I wiped my face on my sleeve. "Dad, how did you

even get here? Mom said you followed me to Baton Rouge. She set off a bomb to scare you away —"

"Derek, your mother's gone," he cut in coldly. "Never mind her."

"Gone? Gone where? Dad —"

"Listen!" he snapped. The battle quieted for a moment. He looked at me carefully. "You know about me," he said. "Don't you?"

Without thinking, I slid down next to him and touched his bandaged arm. He didn't resist. I unwrapped the stained swaths of cloth. The stump was black, dry.

No blood.

My heart sank. My father was someone else.

"You died on land," I said. "You're decaying."

"At Bordelon Gap. I saw a man fall. I needed to return." He wrapped his arm again.

"You saw my *father* fall," I said.

"I had to come back. I was needed here."

"But when this all started, you told me to find Abby," I said. "You told me about the First. You helped me escape from Cane in New Orleans. You tried to save the tourists in Bayou Malpierre. You fought the dead guys. You're on my side —"

"I'm on *my* side," he said quietly.

That was it.

"You're K!" I should have known. It all made sense. And I felt a surge of hope.

"You're not just on your own side. In the sub, you helped Ulysses. You saved him from the First. Did you come to help Ulysses now?" I was still talking about Ulysses as if he was someone else.

He nodded slightly. "Like the older boy helped you."

"Right, the way Ronny came to help me," I said. "My brother, Ronny. You remember him. Your son?"

Only Ronny wasn't his son. Or my brother. This man wasn't my father, either. I kept thinking this way, but it was all wrong. What I had thought was a family for years was now only a group of strangers. Dead strangers.

"You were in the bayou," I prompted. "You were there that night. With Mom."

He pushed the wet hair out of his eyes. "I don't remember that so clearly now. That was your father. I remember some things. He followed her and fired shots to keep the dogs away. He never knew what really happened there until after the train accident and I was inside him."

I heard howling from the fields. It wasn't human. We didn't have much time.

"How much does the Legion know?" I asked.

"The First told Cane that you were Ulysses. Everyone needed you to understand the book. But now it's too late. I need it."

"*You* need it?" I said, my voice rising. "What for? Did you save me from that burning building just now so you could get the poem?" I swung the cartridge box behind my back. "You tried to gain my trust just to get the book?"

Did K want the book for what it said, or for some other reason? Was there something else in it that I'd missed?

"They'll take it," he snapped. "You may not get away. I will. I don't want to hurt you, but you need to give me the book. There's no time to explain."

I climbed to my feet. The stable was an inferno now. The howling moved closer, but I couldn't see Cane or any of the others. I had a chance to run for it. Maybe. "No."

"No?" he spat. It was hard to see my dad like this – angry at me. "You care about Abby, don't you?"

Low blow. "Where is she?" I asked.

"The First has her," he said.

"I don't believe you."

"I led you to the book!" my father burst out. "Step

by step. I told you to find the girl, because I knew her mother had been telling her things. She'd know where the book was. And she did!"

A clatter rang out behind us. I spun and tried to run between the boulders, but couldn't find the way out. There was a sudden explosion over our heads. Rocks slammed my shoulder. My bones screamed. More rocks thudded behind me, and more, and more. One struck my knee hard, jamming it against the ground. I saw Cane's face. He was crawling over the boulders toward me.

"Come here!" Dad reached for my arm but caught the strap of the cartridge box instead and tried to pull me to him. When the strap broke, I realized he wasn't pulling me to him at all.

"No!"

He tore the cartridge box from my hands and slid away. "I need it! You'll never get out —"

He was gone, out of the rocks and through the trees, vanishing like a ghost. I was alone.

The howling came closer.

A second explosion boomed. I shielded myself and threw a loose rock in Cane's direction. He ducked, and I dragged myself away as fast as I could.

I got beyond the boulders somehow, stumbling into the open meadow. My knee throbbed. Was it broken? No, just twisted. I could still move it. Hot pain. A sense of something grinding in the joint, liquid, bleeding under the skin.

I heard the howling again. Only it was so close I knew what it was this time. Dogs.

I turned. White forms galloped across the meadow — right at me.

Waldo's bayou dogs.

I heard his voice pierce the pouring rain now, urging them on. They chased me across the field. I fell into a ditch, dragged myself out, tumbled over the stone wall, and hobbled into the woods.

FOURTEEN

Tower Dogs

Ghost dogs. My chubby legs took over. I ran as fast as I could. The dogs gained on me, galloping through the trees. I heard their ravenous cries all the way to the observation tower, with Waldo shrieking and stumbling after them.

I staggered up the wooden stairs, trying to keep myself moving. My kneecap burned. My brain fired and misfired, a mass of sparks and explosions. I couldn't breathe. I couldn't think. I ran on sheer terror.

"I don't have the book!" I cried, but I barely made a sound over the yelping dogs and the pounding rain and the storm of battle.

I reached the top of the stairs and staggered onto the platform. The guide was gone. Good thing. The ghost dogs, loping white shapes, rushed right after me. When I turned and saw them face-to-face, I stood my ground. There was nowhere else to go.

"Come on!" I found myself screaming at them. "Come on!"

Ghosts can't hurt you; I knew that. Not in such small numbers.

They leaped across the platform at me. I didn't move. It took everything I had to stand there. I wanted to duck, hide. But they just blew across me like a frozen wind before vanishing in the rainy air.

Waldo scrambled up the stairs, feeling his way. He charged onto the platform. His stunted body was a wreck. Waldo had aged since he had been translated years before, but he hadn't grown much. Even though his shriveled body looked like a six-year-old's, inside it was the dead soul of a smuggler born two hundred years ago. He reeked of evil.

"I got you, Derek Stone!" he hollered.

I knew what he was after. "I don't have the book."

One-Arm, the train conductor from Bordelon Gap, clambered up the stairs behind Waldo. His face was gray with death. I backed against the railing, hunkered into a crouch.

"I don't have the book," I repeated.

They weren't into conversation.

Waldo lunged, a mad puppet, while the conductor faked to the side and kicked my battered knee. I stifled a cry and fell backward into the log railing. I heard the crack of wood. A sliver cut into my palm. Gunshots rang out on the ground. While my head was turned, I saw torches crossing the field, a dark mass of men heading to Long Bridge, beyond the woods.

I shifted to my right, faked the conductor, crouched left, and kicked his leg out. He went down hard. I knew he wouldn't stay down, but it was something. Then I knocked Waldo in the face with my fist and dodged past him. Spinning around, I took hold of his shoulders from behind.

"What is the First planning?" I yelled. "What will he do?"

"You can't stop the Grand Return," Waldo said smugly. "The First is more powerful than you can imagine. The dead will come. Tonight!"

"I'll stop him!" I cried.

"You bleed!" Waldo squeaked. "He bled —"

"So what? *Tell me* —"

"It's in the book!" he said.

I paused for a second. Bad idea.

One-Arm had found his footing and rushed at me with the guide's log-footed stool. I dodged and kicked Waldo in the shoulder. He wasn't ready, and tumbled backward down the stairs.

He screamed.

I swung around, grabbed hold of the stool, and jabbed it straight back at One-Arm's face. It struck his nose hard, and he let go. With his only good hand, he punched me in the gut, then grabbed my neck with his iron fingers. I felt light-headed.

Was he trying to cut me? To twist my neck until a coil of smoky fog escaped and I was gone? That was how the translated dead left this world for good. I didn't want to be one of them. I struggled to free myself.

All at once, there was a stinking gray cloud rising over us. Smoke. The tower was burning.

With one hand clawing at his, I bashed my other hand into the stump of the conductor's arm. He gargled in his throat and staggered back, freeing me for a minute. I looked over the railing. Cane was setting the wooden legs of the tower on fire with a pair of blazing torches.

"Cane! No!" One-Arm screamed. "I'm up here!"

The arsonist's face was as blank as Waldo's. The bayou boy was curled on the ground, but he looked up and laughed as if his blind eyes saw the fire and liked it.

One-Arm swung once more at me, pounding my bad ear, before he turned and jumped down the stairs, taking them three or four at a time. Cane didn't wait. He thrust both torches onto the stairs, then stepped away from the tower to watch the flames rise.

I was going to die. I was going to end right there. Except that I couldn't.

A word came to me, and time slowed. A single word. I wasn't sure if I'd thought of it or if *he'd* thought of it. Ulysses. But there it was.

Rope.

Had it come from the mind of the soldier seasoned by battle in the afterlife? Had it come from the leader of the resistance?

Rope.

Or had it come from Derek Stone? Chubby Derek from New Orleans?

Or . . . had it come from some new place? Ulysses as Derek? Derek as Ulysses?

Was this what I was becoming? Both of us?

Time returned to its normal speed. As the flames rose through the tower, barely slowed by the pouring rain, I turned.

The bell rope. Even as I grabbed it with both hands and pulled it quickly up through the tower, I knew the next step. I'd toss it over the side opposite Cane and Waldo. It wasn't long enough to reach the ground, but it was close. I'd have to jump and run.

Jump and run? Was I insane? That was Ulysses talking. I wasn't that brave. I'd fall to my death or have rope burns so bad I'd want to be dead.

But I didn't have a choice.

I dragged the heavy rope to the railing and flung it over the side. Both knees burned now. I heard them grinding as I wound my hands and arms around the rope and began to climb down.

What a heavy mess I was! Still, not as heavy as a week ago.

Fire leaped up the tower. The heat was incredible, but I spotted a path south through the woods and up the river to the manufactory. Thinking ahead already, as if I really would escape.

Ulysses had used the *Phantom* to close the Wound; I was sure of it. The book told how, and the book was gone, but the poem was in my brain. It had to be. I'd written it!

Cane circled the tower, looking past me, trying to see me at the top through all the smoke. *Moron.*

No, good moron. Keep looking up!

I reached the end of the rope and was still dangling about fifteen feet above the ground. My hands stung. The fire, still not on the back side of the tower, leaped straight up. The smoke and flames obscured me. I dangled like an idiot, trying to shorten the distance between me and the ground. Was I really going to jump?

The decision was made for me when the rope burned through at the railing, and I fell. I slammed to the ground. It was not soft. My left knee turned in. I screamed.

Cane was there in a flash, his eyes glinting. I wailed like an animal, and he yanked me up from the ground, one arm around my neck, the other jabbing my back again and again. I couldn't breathe. It couldn't happen this way! I had too much to do! Not like this!

Then a sharp blow, and my spine rang like a chime. I fell like a lead weight.

I had been captured.

Taken, as Cane had promised so long ago.

FIFTEEN

Shroud

My eyes wouldn't open. My mouth tasted like dirty coins. Blood. And wafting past me from somewhere, the faint odor of chemicals I'd smelled earlier in the cemetery.

Chemicals meant the First. And the First had Abby.

My hands were bound behind me. Moving my jaw, I realized that my mouth was sealed. My eyes were covered, my ears under a thick bandage.

I tried to yell. That hurt plenty, and it didn't do any good. The sound came rushing back at me, muffled.

"Shhh," was the reply.

Had I imagined it?

There was no other noise except a low grinding far below me and the *thump-thump-thump* of something closer.

I struggled in and out of consciousness. The poem drifted into and across my mind, like tidewater at the shore. The unfinished story.

Confusion reigns as we approach the gaping Wound;
I steer and steer and steer and

A thicker chemical smell came over me, making me nauseous. Crackling light appeared beyond my bandages. I felt something cold in the air and heard hissing voices. I tried to yell again. No answer. My legs were bent, unmoving. I realized that I was sitting in a chair. How many hours had passed? My weight heaved side to side. The floor was moving.

Was I on a ship?

I wedged open my lips and sucked in. My mouth filled with rags. I bit them — disgusting — and pulled them farther into my mouth with my teeth, gnawing the fabric. I expected someone to notice at any second. No one did. I ground the rags with my teeth again and again until I heard the tear of gauze. The bandage loosened, unwound from my mouth, eyes, and ears like a shroud, and peeled away.

Seconds went by. Nothing.

Gingerly, I opened one eye. Everything was a blur and my head ached, even though the light was dirty and dim. It felt like my eyes had been pressed back into my skull. Who knew how long they'd been wrapped tight? I wanted to rub them, but my hands were tied solidly. I shook my head once, twice, and the rest of my bandages slid off. They lay in my lap, bloody, like the first page of Ulysses' poem.

I blinked a little blurriness away and slowly took in the room. It was narrow, but long. Waldo Fouks sat on an oil drum in the far corner, banging his shrunken feet against the side — *thump-thump-thump*. He seemed oblivious.

But he was my guard. I sat very still.

Humming to himself, Waldo toyed with a furry shape that squirmed between his hands. He couldn't see, but he sensed everything, weirdly, inhumanly. All at once, his hands flew furiously. The thing was trying to escape. Waldo's face tensed and his fingers tightened. A little cry came from his lap, and the thing with fur went still. Waldo opened his hands and the shape thudded to the floor.

The boy shrugged and wiped his palms on his pants.

It was a rat.

I thought of the bag of rats Ronny had brought home from his job at the middle school days before, when this insanity had started. Had it been only days?

Twisting my hands over and over, trying silently to loosen the ties, I focused my swollen eyes on the blank gray walls around me. Riveted wall seams, the smell of oil, the incessant grinding far below. It was a ship, all right.

Suddenly turning his dead eyes to me, Waldo

tensed. "You're breathing louder now than before. You got free from your mouth gag, didn't you?"

"Shut up," I said, hurting too much to mince words.

"Whoo-oo!" he sang. "Ulysses is a toughie! You wait." He started thumping his feet against the drum again, but didn't get up.

I bent one hand around to my back pocket, arched up, and dug into the pocket as quietly as I could. Why hadn't I used the knife when Cane was attacking me? Why had I forgotten I had it? Soldiers don't forget. That meant Derek was still with me.

I guess I liked that.

Using two fingers of my left hand like a pair of tongs, I dragged the knife from my pocket. That alone took a few minutes. When it finally reached the lip of my pocket, it slid and nearly dropped to the floor. I clamped my fingers painfully and saved it from falling. It was almost as hard to get the blade out, but I jacked it open. Gripping the handle as best I could, I slowly began to saw the rope on my right wrist. I'd seen it on TV a hundred times. It actually worked. The people at the museum had kept the old blade sharp. I only missed the rope three times, slashing myself lightly. I almost didn't even notice.

Five minutes, ten minutes, fifteen minutes later, the rope frayed and fell away. I was free.

Waldo's head jerked up. "You wouldn't be trying to escape now, would you?" He hopped down to the floor and turned on me with those dead eye sockets. "There's plenty of strength in these little arms."

I tried to rise quietly to my feet, but Waldo leaped at me with his bony hands extended. I leaned to one side and elbowed him in the neck. He went down in a heap, falling onto the rat. I shoved the oil drum on top of him. Waldo went still.

I froze and looked at his slack, open mouth. What had I done to him?

I turned away and slid out the door into a gray hallway, long and unlit, and forgot about Waldo Fouks.

Abby was on the boat somewhere. My father had said that the First had her. Or K had said it. Or whoever he was. Of course, he could have been lying. He'd tricked me into thinking he was trying to save me. He'd only wanted the book.

I made my way past three, four doors, trying to steady myself on the swaying floor. All at once, something came over me like a dark wave. This was what Ronny had felt in the cemetery, too. I knew it. It sucked away whatever life was in me — and there wasn't much — and replaced it with . . . nothing.

It was him. The First was on the ship.

A deep rumble of engines reverberated under my feet. We were moving. I smelled more chemicals. And something else . . . explosives.

How did I know what explosives smelled like? Maybe it was Ulysses who knew. But what was the difference?

At the end of the hall I saw an open hatch, and beyond it a set of iron stairs. Stepping through the hatch, I peered through a cracked door to my right. I could see that it was late afternoon already, maybe later. How long had I been out? And then I spotted them — what looked like rocket launchers set out on the lower deck of the ship. Firework launchers. I was on the fireworks dredger of Dicky Meade.

Suddenly, my mind connected the dots — some of the dots, anyway. Fireworks. Explosives. What if the hold was packed with explosives to blow the Wound wide open and begin the Grand Return?

Was that how it would happen?

Once the fireworks started, the end would come quickly and harshly. I had to be ready.

Was that right?

Some kind of instinct took over. I made my way up to the top deck of the cabin. It was almost funny how I moved like a snake now, low and fast. This body was thinner, leaner than ever. That, and it had the soul of a soldier, Ulysses Longtemps. What a team!

I needed to stop joking around and just move.

A cabin door appeared on my left. Somehow I knew that Abby was in there.

My senses were electric now. I pulled on the door. Locked. I placed both hands on the hatch handle and tried to turn it. Not an inch. I pulled out the knife.

Ulysses may have been pointing the way, but Derek knew Abby. This was both of us working as one. I finally understood what he'd meant.

Thus boy-I-was and man-I-am combined.

I was being both. Ulysses and Derek. One haunting the other.

I shoved the thick blade into the lock, then turned. The blade tip snapped off, and my hand shook. *Saber broken . . .*

But it had opened the lock.

With all my strength, I pushed open the door. It flung wide. I saw a lamp on top of a bare metal desk and, strangely, a giant fishless aquarium against one wall. Water sloshed over its edges whenever the boat rocked.

Abby was lying motionless on a flat table, bound, eyes wrapped in bandages just like mine had been. Her leg was cut.

"Abby, I'm here —" I started.

My chest was crushed by massive arms from behind. I cried out.

It was Cane.

I had walked into it. Abby was the bait.

My heart hammered in my ears, but over it I heard a squeak of wooden wheels on the iron floor. A wheelchair entered the cabin. The whole room filled with the smell of bitter chemicals.

The First.

The tiny form of a man sat in the chair. At least, I thought he was a man. Was this Dicky Meade? He must have been in his nineties. He was shrunken, a parody of a human, a bag of clothes with a barely fleshed skull wobbling on top. Wisps of tangled white hair cobwebbed his scalp. When he managed to lift his head, his skin sagged. It had the look of wax paper. You could read through it.

Not that you'd want to.

"Let her go," I said. Cane squeezed harder around my chest. I almost fainted. The thing in the chair said nothing.

He wheeled himself slowly over to the aquarium and muttered to Cane. One arm unwound from me but was back before I could move. There was a sound of gears grinding, and a harness — all straps and wires — came down from the ceiling over the chair.

Slipping his upper body into it, the First was

hoisted out of his chair, pulleys and electric winches squealing. His useless legs fluttered under him like rags.

It was disgusting.

Hanging in the sling, he was lowered into the water tank.

Minutes went by silently, except for the sounds of dead men on the deck below, setting up the fireworks. After being submerged in the tank for a while, the old man was hoisted up and settled back into the wheelchair, dripping all over the floor. The water ran off him quickly. It seemed to help him breathe, somehow.

The old thing turned his eyes to me. His left eye looked like a pool of filthy oil. His right one was a pale marble, false, a ball bearing that drifted around the socket, sometimes arcing up into his forehead when his face was down, sometimes scanning off to the side.

"It's time for this body to go," he said. I wasn't sure if he was speaking to me. "I needed it for tonight, but now I must have new blood."

"Let her go," I said, glancing over at Abby. It was lame, but I didn't want to play word games. "Let her go," I repeated in the same tone. I sounded either really determined, or totally crazy.

The First didn't speak at once. Good. I could use some extra time. Extra time for what, I wasn't sure. To try to understand what was happening.

"It's a long time, a hundred and forty-four years," he said finally. "Body after body turning worthless as husks. Through the years, I bled less and less. I had to drench myself to stay moving, until Dicky Meade. Old, senile coot! I finally entered him in 1982. That started my real work on the river." He paused for a minute, almost thoughtfully. "You take a little of each of them with you when you move on."

No kidding. I was the poster boy for that.

"Then, ten years ago, my dredging cracked open the vault of death. A tiny rip where the veil was weakest, worn through by hundreds of centuries to the barest gauze between life and death. Remember that, ten years ago?"

I remembered.

"A soul came through, on a mission. It traveled through the water that connects every inch of this earth, all the way down to that stinking bayou. I sensed that soul. I knew, someday, it would come for me. I met him once. On the other side."

Creepy as it all was, I knew who he was talking about.

"Ulysses," I said.

"Y-y-you," he whispered fiercely, his voice dripping with loathing. "That first opening in 1864 gave us hope. We could escape our torture in the afterlife. I did escape, but before my men could follow, you closed the rip."

"So why didn't you cut me in the bayou ten years ago?" I asked. "You were there. You knew then who I was supposed to be."

The First sat very still. "When I sensed who took over your body in the bayou," he said, "I remembered that there was . . . a book. I needed it. You had to grow up and find the book. And I had to be patient.

"After the train crash, you began to move. I knew it would come to you, where your book was, how to find it, what it meant. Ulysses was brilliant — *you* were brilliant. You saw the Wound and knew exactly how to close it. But the book is so much more to me."

All this time, Abby hadn't stirred. Now her head shifted. She coughed, then went still again.

Meade wheeled over to a steel bookcase behind the desk. There were rows of bottled chemicals lined up there. He opened one and sniffed it. The smell was overpowering.

"I bled, for a while," he mused, closing the bottle again. "What I would give to have that blood again. It doesn't belong to any of the bodies. It's not his blood, you know. Not Tom Bell's. It's mine."

"What?" My head spun.

"No, no," he said, almost in a whisper. "That blood came with me. The soul I was is *in* that blood. There's no more left. The book is the only place now."

What could he possibly mean?

"I don't have the book," I said.

"But where is the book?" he pressed. "You see, that's what I want to know. Where it is, so I can have it."

It struck like lightning. Had my father — K — stolen the book to keep it away from the First? Had he *not* tricked me?

"It's . . . it's lost," I said.

The First made a noise in his throat and began to paw his left ear, smoothing his few strands of hair over it. He did this again and again, like Fat Henry in the barn and Old Tom in the *Phantom,* two other bodies the First had translated into.

"Since I don't have the book — yet —" the old man began calmly, pulling a broken saber from a desk drawer.

I trembled. Was this Ulysses' saber? After so many years? So many deaths?

"You do it," he said, holding the saber out toward me.

"Do what?"

"The blade must be the same," he said, motioning

to Abby with the broken saber. "It's why I have stayed so long. You do it. I'll tell you how."

What?

This crazy old guy expected me to use the broken saber on Abby? He wanted to translate into her, and I was supposed to . . . ? I couldn't even think.

"I'll find the book," I said, barely able to speak. My chest ached. I tried to steady myself, but Cane's grip on me was iron.

The old man's voice was hollow, deep, and barely controlled, seething with anger.

"Too late now," he said. "You're a surgeon. You'll do it just right."

And then it hit me.

The blood. He wanted the blood from the book. It was his. Something — one of those chemicals? — would draw his blood out of the paper, and he would . . . what? Take it in somehow? And he would live longer?

I looked around frantically for something to stall him a little more. Then, on the shelf behind his head, I saw the spine of a book I knew.

Afterlives by Tomas Deak.

So. The First had learned from it, too.

The more similar the manner of death, the better the fit. The less similar, the less the fit.

"Meade," I said. No one heard me, because at that moment, two men in scuba suits appeared in the doorway.

The First turned to them. "The stern hull is half a foot thick," he said. "You sure you have enough?"

The men nodded once and left.

"Meade —" I said again.

"It all starts now," the old man said, his mouth barely moving. The harness lifted him up. He leaned over Abby and removed her bandages, leaving her mouth stuffed with rags.

She blinked and saw me. Her eyes were frantic. She tried to scream. An awful, muffled sound.

Then I heard it: a low noise. Familiar. A voice deeper than human voices. It was the sound I'd first heard back in New Orleans the day Ronny had returned. The same voice I'd heard in the manufactory.

"Meade!" I said sharply, trying to stall for a few more minutes.

The old man turned his cadaverous face to me.

"K will come," I said. "He'll stop you. He . . . told me."

Meade's eyes rolled over me from side to side, like dead fingers stroking my cheek. He said nothing.

"Or my mother," I went on. "She'll find you —"

"Your mother!" he spat suddenly. "She paralyzed me! She broke my spine in the bayou. That's why I'm in this wheelchair!" He plunged the saber into his leg, and my stomach flipped. He sounded frantic now, frenzied. "You see? No blood left! Soon you'll be like me. You're the only other one who bled, you know."

"Why?" I demanded, my voice hoarse. "Why me?"

"We're charmed; we'll live long," he said, not answering. "But now I'm dry. I need my blood!"

I heard that familiar voice on the stairs below. With all my strength, I kicked back at Cane's knee. It was enough. The giant lurched to the side. I slipped from his grasp and rushed at Meade, knocking his skeletal hands away from Abby. He howled and slashed at me with the saber, cutting my arm. Blood rose along the gash. But nowhere near as much as there should have been.

Was I already changing?

Abby saw the cut. Her eyes flashed.

And then the voice I'd heard before reached the door. Hinges squealed as the door blew open. The lamp exploded. The room went dark.

SIXTEEN

The Hour of Magical Thinking

"Cut him!" the old man shouted in the dark. I heard him dangling loosely in his harness. "Forget the blood, just cut —"

"Derek, get down!" It was Ronny.

I ducked, and he swung a pipe. Cane yelled when it hit his thick flesh. Chairs crashed around me. Ronny struck again.

Splashing echoed inside the cabin, and a sharp odor surrounded me. Gasoline. My arm was wrenched toward the door by cold fingers. The room went yellow with flame. Cane's face was aglow.

Ronny freed Abby from the table. She swung her legs to the floor, but her wounded leg twisted. Ronny pulled her up in his arms and ran from the room. I was right behind.

Together, we tramped down the metal stairs and outside. Rain still battered the iron deck. I slipped but got up quickly. Three Legion soldiers rushed at us from behind the firework launchers. Ronny shoved

Abby over to me, then used the pipe in his hand like an ax. The soldiers dropped to their knees, and Ronny dragged us past the cabin toward the back of the boat.

Cane limped down the stairs, smoldering, following us. Abby jerked herself away from me. "I can . . . I can . . . walk."

"Try to run," said Ronny. "Here they come!" He pulled us to the railing and dived off the side of the boat, taking both of us with him.

We sank into the black river. I flailed until I reached the surface. I hated the water, but my arms wouldn't stop moving.

Gunshots pounded the waves. It was nearing evening and too dark to aim for anything. Abby's hand was tight on my arm as we let the current carry us downstream. Darkness and smoke covered us, and the shooting stopped. We made our way to the western bank and pulled ourselves up.

Torches lit Bloody Meadow. A skirmish was in full force in the woods to the north. The air filled with the sound of clashing blades, the pop-popping of muskets, and under it all, sinister voices.

"We're not done," Ronny said, scanning the field above us and wringing out his shirt. "As soon as the fireworks start, we're in even bigger trouble."

I thought back to the wreck of the *Eastport*, remembered the *Phantom* diving. . . .

"I have to go to the manufactory," I said. "Now. The *Phantom* —"

Ronny screwed up his face. "What do you think you're going to do there? Look, I don't know what kind of thing you have going with the ghosts, but we need more men —"

"Keep it down!" Abby whispered at us. She scrambled into the edge of the woods and fell to her knees, trying to catch her breath.

I knew time was running out. I pulled Ronny away so she couldn't hear. "I have to tell you something. . . ."

The way he looked at me, I could tell that he knew, right at that moment.

"I . . . died . . . in the bayou," I said quietly. "Ten years ago. Ulysses . . . he came into me. . . ."

He nodded, eyes down. "Your mother. She told you at Amaranthia?"

I think the patch on his cheek grew when I said yes. Tears welled in his eyes, but he didn't cry. He took it like a soldier told of the death of a friend. Like Ulysses when he saw Tom Bell die. Like me when I'd thought Ronny had died. Like Abby with her mother.

"Okay, then," he said. And that was it. He understood.

The meadow lit up with gunfire. Ronny called Abby and pulled me by the shirt to the southern end of Cross Crag. We weaved among the stones as a swarm of bullets pinged off the boulders all around us.

I couldn't believe the stupid reenactment was still going on. The confusing terrain kept different groups of men from knowing what was happening with the others. Already translations in the wet ground had swelled the Legion. There were hundreds more than those who'd come in the trucks. Their voices clanged in my ears.

Ronny peeked over the stones, but gunfire forced him back down. He punched his fist into his palm.

"What's the matter?" I said.

"What's n-not the matter? Look at it. We need to s-s-stop them. I t-told you. We need more men —"

"What men?" said Abby, turning to him. "There's only us."

"We have to stop the Grand Return!" Ronny snapped. "I c-can put stuff together. The explosives on that boat are going to rip a hole in the Wound so huge that there will be no way to close it. The Legion will push two thousand men into the water, the

Wound will open, and the Grand Return will happen."

"Ulysses stopped it with the submarine the first time," I said. "I'm sure he did."

"And what are you going to do?" Ronny sputtered. "T-take it into the r-river? You thought three hundred Legion soldiers was bad? Try thousands. After that, m-millions. That's how m-many will come if the Wound is blown open!"

Ronny was stomping back and forth down one of the alleys of the Crag. "We need men," he repeated. "Hundreds, at least. More."

"What am I supposed to do?" I said. "I can't make them magically appear."

"You c-c-can!" said Ronny. He grabbed me by the shoulders. His breath was horrible, rotten. "You can! Call them from the afterlife. You see their ghosts. Call up their souls!"

"Are you mental?" said Abby. "How can Derek do that?"

But I knew what Ronny meant.

After death, the soul resides exclusively in the afterlife — unless it returns in physical form. I knew what he meant, but the idea was horrifying. I couldn't force myself to connect the dots. "Ronny, that's crazy *and* impossible —"

"There's no other way!" he cried. "You saw what kind of beast the First is."

"But how can I?"

"You know how!" he yelled. "The ambush on the bridge. I heard the guide talking. You know about it. It was your troop. You were there when it happened! The souls could find their way there — if you call them."

Abby shook her head. "Ronny, calm down. You're talking crazy."

"Use the ambush," Ronny said, ignoring her and grabbing my shirt in his cold fist. "Use it to bring your troop back. They're loyal to you. They'll follow you anywhere! The ambush will happen again if you make it happen."

"What are you saying?" asked Abby.

Ronny let out a yell. "The souls of your old troop, Ulysses! They have to translate into the reenactors! There's no other way!" He was right up in my face. "Forget D-Derek. We need Ulysses n-n-now."

"No," I said. It was barely a whisper. "I can't do that!"

"You have to!" Ronny burst out. "You're their captain! You have a responsibility to everyone. Tell her!"

He flashed an angry look at Abby.

"What?" Abby demanded. "What is he talking about?"

"I . . . I . . ." I was frozen.

Ronny tore his hand away from my shirt. "I can't sit around and watch this happen. I'm going to try to lead the reenactors away from the river." He gave me a hard look. "You're Ulysses Longtemps. Be a hero again."

Then he was gone.

I stood in the rain, looking after him, and I knew deep inside that there was no other way.

"What was *that* all about?" Abby said. I just took her arm and pulled her with me through the rocks. The sounds of battle were all around us, but the fireworks hadn't started yet.

"We're going to the Long Bridge," I said.

"Derek, what did Ronny mean?" said Abby. "He was kidding when he called you Ulysses, right? Because of the poem?"

I didn't answer. Couldn't. I pushed through the outlying woods to the winding wagon path. A troop of reenactors saw us and called out. But by the time Abby tried to warn them, they had already hastened along a stone wall, away from the path. They didn't hear.

I marched faster in the drenching rain, breathing hard. The rain was its own sort of battle, pelting the road. It covered my face, washing the blood from my arm. The blood that made me special. The blood that was already drying up.

I paused in the center of Swamp Road. Abby looked around, trying to figure out which direction I was going in next. But I was already there. The Ghost Road. The road that led all the way to Ulysses' death.

"Come out," I said. "I'm here." I spoke too softly, almost in a whisper — like I had spoken at the bayou and everywhere else. Too softly.

"Come out!" Louder now.

"Derek," Abby said, "who are you talking to? Tell me I didn't really hear what I heard. Tell me, Derek."

I spun around to face her. This was it.

"Abby, I'm dead."

She stepped back. "No . . ."

"I'm dead," I repeated, rain dripping down my face.

"You're not," she said quietly. "Derek, please. It's scary enough —"

"It's what my mother told me at Amaranthia. I'm like Ronny. That's what this is all about. I'm the author of that poem. *I'm* the author. I wrote it in 1864. I'm Ulysses Perceval Longtemps. He translated into me in the bayou when I was four —"

She wasn't having any of it. "No! You only have to read the poem to find out what to do, but now that it's gone, you're getting scared. You're Derek Stone."

"Abby —"

"No! You shut up! Just shut up!" Her face was wild, dripping in the rain, her eyes on fire.

"Abby, I'm sorry. Ulysses came back ten years ago, because he needed to close the Wound. Now I have to call the others back to help me close it again. Ronny's right. We need them to help us win this war. Otherwise, we don't stand a chance."

She was frantic now, her hands clamped over her ears.

"It has to be done," I said. "I know what I'm doing."

"You don't!" she pleaded. "Even if Ulysses . . . *did* do that . . . Even if he did translate into you when you were small, it was a horrible thing, a terrible thing. He was a soldier. He had to do it. But not you! You're still Derek. I don't know Ulysses. I know Derek, and I wouldn't be here unless Derek is still here —"

"I *am* still here!" I shouted at her. "I am. But it's time for Ulysses to come out."

Musket shots pinged the stone wall to our left. I hurried down the road. I heard water splashing all around us.

"I have to hurry, before the fireworks start."

"Derek, please don't . . . ," Abby said.

But she stayed right next to me.

I kept on toward the Long Bridge. The road wound past the barn. I heard a voice, saw a shape in its murky shadows, but didn't let on to Abby. In my mind, I said one word.

Rope.

The shape saw me, somehow understood the word, then moved off into the darkness. It wasn't K. It wasn't Ronny. It was Madeline Donner.

I needed her help.

Maybe sensing her mother, Abby scanned the trees, saw nothing, and struggled to keep up with my wild marching, still arguing with me.

I stopped on the road and tried again. "You said you were ready. Well, now I'm here. I need you. I'll show you the way. Come out!"

This time they came.

SEVENTEEN

On the Long Bridge

They came from the woods, from the sunken ground, from ditches, from hillocks, from behind stone walls. Four hundred came, splashing the flooded ground.

They were the troops who had fought with me in 1864, ghosts of the long dead. I knew they were good men. They wouldn't want to do what I was planning to ask, but they came when I called them.

Hundreds of ghosts massed in the road, every eye fixed on me. I knew them all. They were the men I'd lost at the Long Bridge during the Battle of Cemetery Bend. I recognized some of them from the barn earlier, only now I knew their names.

Every one.

"I need your souls to return," I announced.

A ripple of something went through the ghosts. Fear? Disgust?

Maybe.

But they didn't leave. I knew what I was asking of them. These ghosts were only the shadows of dead souls residing in the afterlife. I needed their souls to create a physical army to fight the Legion here and now. I was asking them to do what good souls had always refused to do — to translate.

"I need your souls to return," I said again.

This time, there was no movement among the ghosts, until Jem stepped out in front of them. He looked from face to face among the troops, and then at me.

"We'll do whatever you say, Captain."

My heart broke, knowing what I was asking.

Abby shivered beside me. "They're going to do it, aren't they?"

I nodded. "To the bridge!"

I turned and marched down the road. Four hundred ghosts followed me past the woods, the barn, the stone walls, to the site of their terrible death at the old stone bridge.

"Derek, don't," Abby said, stumbling along with me. "This is insane. It's wrong. Please . . ."

Her eyes were dark. She could have abandoned me, knowing who I was and what I planned to do. But just like the four hundred ghosts, she stayed.

By some amazing stroke of luck, the fireworks hadn't

started yet. The barge hadn't moved since we'd escaped it. As soon as it did, I would have to be down there, underwater in the *Phantom.* I hoped Ulysses' words would come to me then, but first I had to do this.

If I was losing my humanity, so be it. I was already dead. This had to be done, and there was no one else who could do it. That's what I told myself, anyway.

"Hurry!" I shouted over my shoulder, and the ghost troops sped up to match my stride.

Abby walked behind me silently. I wondered if she knew about her mother's role in all of this. She would soon.

We marched farther down the road among the trees, and there it was — the Long Bridge. Its seven stony arches leaped over the rushing water. I stopped.

The ghosts faded from the air as if they were no more than mist, and the water below the bridge began thrashing. It splashed and boiled with their waiting souls, willing to return if I needed them. I felt like some kind of creepy sorcerer, raising the dead in the dark, cold rain.

But what choice did I have? "Be ready!"

A minute passed. Two minutes.

"What's happening?" Abby asked me. All she could see was an empty bridge. "Are the ghosts gone?"

At that moment, Madeline Donner staggered out

of the woods, carrying the singed bell rope from the tower in her hands.

Abby gasped when she saw her mother. She wanted to go to her, but I held her back. She turned and saw no surprise on my face. "Derek, why is she here?"

"I told her to come."

Like Ronny, Madeline Donner knew that the only way to battle the Legion was with physical force. Ghosts couldn't do much against dead souls in bodies. They'd routed the Legion at Amaranthia, but that had only been temporary. We needed to stop the Legion here — for good — or there would be no stopping them anywhere.

"The rope!" I cried. Abby's mother strung it quickly across the bridge, pulled it taut, then loosened it with one end still in her hands.

I heard horses' hooves thundering through the woods.

Chains meant to bind, tore hooves asunder. We charged
Across the bridge. A few of us — no more — passed by
Before those chains pulled taut across the stone,
And sent both horse and man to ambush and to death below.
I hear their screams each hour since.

In my mind I saw the reenactors, acting like children riding to play war. They had no idea. But they were heading right for the Legion anyway. They were dead either way. At least now, my men would return in them to fight.

"I'm going," said Abby. She twisted from my grip and ran to her mother. Madeline's face was blank, but she lifted her frail hands to her daughter. It wouldn't last. The horses were coming. I knew what Abby's mother would do.

It would happen like this:

The cavalry bursts from the woods toward the bridge.

"Derek!" Abby cries. Her mother turns away, nearly lifeless, one last mission in her. Madeline Donner pulls the rope tight across the bridge.

Abby muffles a scream as the first riders shout, their horses' hooves catching the rope, which tangles the frightened beasts.

Six horses fall to the stones, beginning a horrifying chain collision. Pushed forward by the stampeding horses, the whole troop crashes off the sides of the bridge. Five riders, forty, two hundred hurtling into the water, to the souls waiting below.

That ambush on the bridge would be the same as it was in April 1864. I remembered it then. Except that what follows this time is the marching of boots, the thumping of hooves, the assembling of soldiers — four hundred dead good men to fight the Legion.

And I will lead them.

But that wasn't the way it happened.

My memory, that messed-up jumble, spit out one line of the poem again, and everything changed.

I hear their screams each hour since.

To a chorus of wild yells, the first horses galloped out of the woods, riders driving them as fast as they would go. But the eyes of the reenactors were filled with horror. This was no fake battle.

Was I really a killer, like the First? No better than that?

"No!" I shouted.

I jumped for Madeline Donner, pushed Abby away, and sent her mother running off the bridge. The rope fell slack to the ground.

The horses streamed across the bridge in one long line. Four hundred horses thundered past me and galloped off into the fog.

The Long Bridge massacre did not happen again.

I'd failed.

We didn't have those four hundred soldiers now. I couldn't kill innocent men. The Legion would have at least three times as many men soon, probably ten times.

We had only Ronny and Abby and me.

I watched the last of the horses ride away in the rain and wondered if the riders would survive the Legion. I hoped so. But hope dies quickly on the battlefield.

A minute later, the ghosts returned to the bridge. Jem stepped toward me, looking at me questioningly.

Something rose in me just then. Call it courage. Or honor. Or insanity. But looking into the faces of my troops, I felt we could *still* fight the dead. We could push them to the river and back into the Wound. It was possible. I'd seen it at Amaranthia. Me and a troop of ghosts.

"We can do this! If you have any love for the world you left, then take arms now. Push the Legion to the river!"

The ghosts' eyes — every one — were fixed on me. I knew I had them.

"You remember the first time we fought this battle, so you know that in a little while, I won't be here. The *Phantom* will take me away. But don't be afraid! Hope, if it exists, will lead us to victory!"

I was all flowery in spite of myself. I spoke like the poem now.

The ghosts made a sound that rumbled through my bones. They were ready.

Abby put her hand in mine and held tight.

"Are you ready?" I called. The sound from the ghosts grew louder. Abby's hand shook.

The ghosts gathered close. I could feel a spark of energy, like a storm brewing.

"Are you ready?"

The river below the bridge shrieked. Ghost horses, hundreds of them, galloped up from the water, streaming wet. My men were on them in an instant.

"Draw the Legion to the river!" I shouted. "Push them into the water!"

Their reply was a deafening roar of wind, cold and strong. Rain fell like sheets of iron and coiled around the mounted ghosts. The storm of ghosts shot away from the bridge and galloped through the woods, toppling trees with its force.

I watched them fly up to the crest of the field, then turned on my heels.

I hasten now. The end is coming near.

Without a second thought, I ran as fast as I could to the little black building on the shore.

EIGHTEEN

Lung of Iron

I slogged through the pine swamps, through the low growth and the mud. Abby was right behind me.

I tried to piece together a plan as I walked, but I felt like a ghost tethered to its haunting place. I kept going around and around the same point.

Explosives.

Only a huge explosion could cauterize the opening between the worlds. Ulysses' training as a surgeon taught me about closing wounds. Sealing the Wound — cauterizing it — was the opposite of enlarging the Wound. Both were violent actions, but they had opposite results.

One act saved our world. The other doomed it.

I had no explosives, but the First did. The hull of the dredger was filled with them. He'd use them to blast the Wound open even wider. I'd use them to seal it closed forever. Easy enough, right?

Sure. No problem. But how was I supposed to do that?

All I knew was that the poem ended with Ulysses in the *Phantom,* approaching the Wound. That was where it had all happened then, so that was where it would have to happen now.

The sky burst with light.

This was followed by a thunderous explosion that shook the air. The fireworks had begun. I had minutes. I ran faster, to the streets of Cemetery Bend and right to the shore. Abby stayed close behind me. She knew the worst and still followed me.

When I got near the manufactory, I could see that it was a smoldering shell pouring black smoke into the gray sky. Cane had done his job here.

Firefighters scrambled up and down the sides of the building with hoses and axes, but the damage was already done. I was surprised to see Professor Bloom stomping around in a rage. She hadn't gone back to New Orleans after all.

My bad ear ached suddenly. Waldo Fouks was lurking in the shadows; I could feel it. What would it take to stop the little creep?

"Derek, look!" said Abby. "The fireworks are coming faster now."

"I'm out of time," I said. "The *Phantom* is in the tank. Professor Bloom said you can get to it only from underneath. You'd better leave."

"Not a chance," she said. "We're doing this together."

Abby worked her way past me, slipping unseen down to the riverbank. Without a word, she dived into the water. I raced to the shore after her.

Waldo must have heard the splash. He stumbled out of hiding, from behind a garage, and shuffled unseeing toward the sound. Toward me.

Professor Bloom turned, on edge. "Who's over there?"

A spotlight whipped around from one of the police cars. Two officers hurried across the parking lot toward me, calling out.

I ran at Waldo, knocking him on his back like an overturned beetle. The policemen yelled, but I ignored them and leaped into the water. It was filthy, thick. I tried to keep my eyes open to see Abby, but couldn't. I hoped she had already found the tank.

I made my way along the shore, then dived deep and groped along the rocky ledge until I felt the smooth side of the metal tank. I knew it was sealed on top but open at the bottom, and it would have protected the submarine from the fire. I still heard Waldo squealing in my head. I dived farther, but the lower edge of the tank wasn't where I thought it would be. I kept reaching deeper and deeper into the water.

Finally, I felt the bottom edge, but I couldn't pull

myself down to slip beneath it and into the tank. My arms ached. My lungs screamed. I had no air left. Then a hand grabbed my wrist and pulled. Abby yanked me under the edge of the tank. I burst through the surface of the water, gasping for air.

"Thanks," I panted. "I was —"

"Save it," Abby said, cutting me off. She was angry. Fine. She might never understand, but she was there with me.

The *Phantom* floated half-submerged in the tank, its top hatch above the water. The air in the tank was hot from the fire.

Without talking, Abby and I raised the iron door on the front of the tank, leaving the way open to enter the river. I threw off the chains holding the *Phantom* in place, and we crawled up the side of the sub. One after the other, we dropped through the hatch.

"This isn't going to kill us, is it?" Abby asked when I lowered the hatch over us and shut it tight.

"You bet it will," I said.

No laugh? Fine. At least she was there.

I grabbed the crank running from the nose to the tail of the sub, and began turning it. The shaft turned the propeller, slowly at first. Abby joined in, and the *Phantom* moved quickly out of the tank and into the river, the hatch still above the water.

. . . playing boats and underboats along the riverbank . . .

The two of us turned the crank as quickly as we could, but I knew that the *Phantom* worked best with as many as six men, not a couple of kids. Never mind that. We had what we had.

I tried not to think about being buried alive, but that was what it felt like in there — an iron coffin. The concave walls didn't leave much elbow room but demanded a lot of elbow *grease* to keep the propeller moving. I dreaded the moment when we would have to submerge the sub entirely.

"We only have one chance to do this," I found myself saying. "Only one chance. One chance . . ."

Abby groaned. "Wait. How many chances?"

"What?"

"Derek!" she snapped. "I get it. But could you *not* be Ulysses for a second and just use the motor? This is not the easiest thing for two people to do, even if I am stronger than you."

I blinked. "Yeah, sorry. Sure. Use the motor."

She had already flipped the switch, and the rear of the sub began to hum. We moved more quickly through the water. The small porthole over the nose showed that we were in the body of the river now. In the sky above was a constant barrage of fireworks. It would be over soon.

We motored, half submerged, for another few minutes.

"We'd better go farther down," Abby said after a while. "You know . . . dive."

I nodded, pulled the lever, and heard the diving fins pivot outside the sub. Water slid all the way up the porthole, and we were under, moving a bit faster now. There was some kind of headlight powered by a set of pedals on the floor near my feet. As long as I kept pedaling, the light was just bright enough to illuminate what was outside the porthole. Even through the dark water, I could see the black hull of the barge in the distance. It had started to move down the western bank of the river, toward the bottom of Bloody Meadow.

I tried to focus. I had to do what Ulysses had done. I didn't have the poem anymore, but if I squeezed every last bit of memory, maybe I'd find the answer I needed. Maybe.

I crank the rotor shaft with all the strength of body I can muster,
Yet only strength of heart will see me through . . .

The sky whitened with bursting fireworks. Far below in the water, small lights — flashlights? — swung around the dredger's stern.

"We need to get over there," I said.

Abby studied the gauges on the wheel in front of

her. "Then we're off course," she said. "We have to go twelve thingies southwest."

"Degrees?" I said.

"Yeah, those."

We were quite a team.

Together, we turned the rudder wheel that many marks. The submarine shifted toward the dredger. There was movement under the stern again.

"What *is* that?" I muttered. Then I saw them: two scuba divers. They had attached something to the hull and were swimming back to a nearby motorboat.

"Abby," I said. She stared out the porthole with me. "When we were on the dredger, the First told the divers that the hull is thick there," I said.

"Is that a bomb?" she said, suddenly sounding panicked. "Did they just put a bomb on the bottom of the big boat?"

I shrugged, thinking out loud: "But if that's the explosive . . . it's so *small*. It won't do anything. . . ."

Abby shook her head. "Maybe it's just to sink the boat. The explosives are on the dredger, in the hold or something, right? What if they're just going to sink the boat because the big explosion will happen when it hits the river bottom?"

Of course she was right.

The rumble of the dredger's engines idled, then died. As we motored closer, we could see the murky bottom of the river below the black hull. Pieces shuttled into place in my head.

"The Wound . . . ," I said. "It must be below the dredger now. Right now." I pressed my face to the glass porthole and searched the dark water. I remembered lines from the poem.

Then all at once, I see a thing — I rush to write it down!

A ledge of stone like a giant's bone —

"There. Look!" I said. We drove the *Phantom* lower in the water, and the rocky ledge Ulysses had seen all those years ago came into view. It was a shelf about seventy-five feet long, narrow, but pure stone; it must have weighed hundreds of tons. It seemed like an outcropping of the guts of the earth itself.

"I can't believe it," Abby breathed.

The bedrock was torn apart where the dredging had opened it. Stress on the rocks had shifted the plates of stone under the riverbed.

My heart thundered in my chest. "Holy —"

The water rocked with an explosion. It was small, but tossed the sub backward and off our course. When the porthole cleared, we saw the dredger tilt suddenly. Water must have been rushing in through the hole made by the explosion.

A second explosion sounded, and the boat began to sink faster.

"They'll blow the Wound wide open!" said Abby, turning to me. Her eyes were wide, pleading. "We don't know what we're doing. Without the book, there's nothing we can do."

"We have to get closer," I said calmly.

"No, we have to get out of here!"

NINETEEN

The Red Stain

It was all happening too fast. The dredger's stern sank deeper. Time was slipping away. And my brain wasn't working. I had no idea how to seal the Wound shut.

"Bring us closer," I said. It was all I could think to do.

"You're out of your mind!" Abby said, but she turned the rudder anyway.

What I saw as we got closer and closer terrified me.

It lay there under the massive ledge: a tear in the earth, as narrow as a sliver but thirty or forty feet long. It looked like fabric — a flimsy fabric separating the worlds — and it was torn, waving like ragged seaweed in the current. Seeing it like this so many years ago must have been the first time he really understood.

Grasping at the Wound to broaden it, to enter here,
Those hungry souls demanding to assault our world!

It stopped my heart. Who were those souls below us? Beauchamp's Butchers? The two thousand evil dead wanting to come back to our world?

"Derek!" Abby screamed, pointing at the dredger.

The big ship sank even more quickly, its bow lifting out of the water now. Its stern aimed for a point just north of the Rift itself. But I knew that that would change as it sank.

"Derek, it's going to blow if it hits anything. We need to get out!"

But my mind was back in the old *Phantom*.

I remembered everything.

Tom kept yelling that he had to make the Wound bigger. Ulysses tried to stop him. Tom fell on him with the saber. K leaped past Ulysses from behind and pushed Tom away. The saber jerked backward, and that all-important blood flew across the cabin and the book.

"I must seal that opening!" cry I. "Cauterize the wound!
I'll wrench the rudder quickly to the crux,
Collapse the hanging ledge upon itself —"

But there was a right place to collapse the hanging ledge upon itself, and a wrong place. The wrong place was where the dredger was heading. It would blast the Wound wide open.

"We have to slow down the ship's fall until we find the right spot," I said suddenly. "We need to ram the dredger!"

"Ram *what*?" Abby said, dropping her hands from the rudder levers. "Are you kidding? I'm turning us around."

"No!" I shouted. I took the rudder from her and steered the *Phantom* right at the sinking boat.

"Derek, we're going to die. . . ."

"I told you we would," I said.

"I thought you were kidding!"

I had hoped I was.

The dredger was pointed almost straight down now. We moved directly under the sinking barge. Suddenly, it thudded down behind our heads like another explosion. It nearly sliced the little submarine in two. The dredger's giant hull ground into our iron shell, buckling the plates and denting the tail — but not puncturing it. Not yet. The massive heft of it pushed us down toward the bottom. It was insane to think we could guide the dredger's massive weight to the right spot. I scoured the riverbed.

Confusion reigns as we approach the gaping Wound;

I steer and steer and steer and

That was how the poem ended. I had no memory after that. "Ulysses discovered exactly what would expand the Wound and what would close it," I said aloud. "But he had no time to write it down."

"Where did he crash it?" Abby asked, urging me. "Is that part of the code?"

The ceiling of the sub quaked as the dredger sank farther. My eyes burned. I needed air.

Then it came to me.

Maybe the poem wasn't a code at all. Maybe the real code was my memory, and Ulysses' poem was like a key. His words would unlock something in me that wasn't even written on his pages!

And of all the lines of the poem, one kept coming back to me:

I'll wrench the rudder quickly to the crux,

Collapse the hanging ledge upon itself —

And suddenly that was it.

Crux.

Ulysses — I — had used the word once before, at the beginning of the poem.

. . . playing boats and underboats along the riverbank

(His dubbed the Crux, *mine* Spectre *was) —*

Crux was the name of the constellation also called the Southern Cross, which only appears in the southern hemisphere. Ulysses knew that. I knew that. Of course, "Crux" meant "Cross," but here — *here* — Ulysses meant it to mean "southern."

I was supposed to look south, to the southernmost edge of the Wound.

I flung the motor in reverse. "Back the other way!"

"You're crazy!" Abby said. "We can't —"

The sub lurched backward, south, the weight of the barge on us.

There, tucked into the riverbed, was a shard of something encrusted with barnacles. Plant fronds waved slowly around it. The thing was unmoving and angular — a slab of old gray iron fused into the rock.

"The *Phantom*," I breathed. "I see it. The original *Phantom*! Abby, we found it! We need to steer there. Abby —"

She muttered something softly and slumped over in her seat.

Our air was gone. Our half hour was done.

I suddenly felt very light-headed.

But no. It couldn't end this way. Not when we were this close. I didn't know where the strength came from, but I locked the rudder in place, as I somehow knew Ulysses had done. Holding my breath, I hammered the hatch open with my bare hands. I had only seconds. Water flooded in. I pulled Abby's limp form with me, away from the enormous hull of the dredger, up through the water to the surface. We left the husk of the replica *Phantom* to push the sinking dredger on top of Ulysses' original.

I kicked as hard as I could and finally broke the surface, knowing then that Ulysses had never made it this far. The *Phantom* had exploded before he reached the surface, and all went black in his head. His body must have washed up later, his book in the cartridge box strapped to his corpse.

Lifting Abby's head above the water, I battled to the shore. She coughed and gasped; then her arms began to move. "Just a little farther . . . ," I huffed.

The air was suddenly filled with the cries of ghosts and the howling of the evil dead. The river thrashed at the foot of Bloody Meadow. It was my troop of untranslated ghosts, pushing the Legion into the water.

Plain old Derek could not have done all this.

But I was more than that now. The ghosts of my troop — a storm — had forced the Legion down the bank and into the river, just like at Amaranthia. Their ghost horses were pure energy, their swords like flames. Maybe that was all the ghosts could do — move things with force.

But it was enough.

My ghosts wouldn't back down. They battered the Legion like a force of nature, pushing them all right over the top of the sinking barge.

Abby and I had almost reached the shore when the river exploded.

The world exploded.

Giant columns of water burst into the air. The river convulsed from below, flying up and out, over and over, and crashing down like boulders upon the battlefield. Then a huge gulf appeared in the river. It was a crater that stretched from bank to bank, sucking water down into it like a vacuum. The wails of the Legion stabbed my ears, as they were drawn down under the surface. Wave after wave crashed. Abby was ripped from my arms, and we were thrown through the water.

My heart stopped, started, stopped again. I watched it all like it was a dream. The river turned white, then black. I was hurtled out of myself and back in and back out again. Miles came and went.

Years came and went.

And still I was moving away away away.

TWENTY

Brothers in Arms

The explosion threw me up and out of the water. I struck the bank hard and hit my head on a rock. Did I bleed? I couldn't tell. I didn't care. I knew that the blood would stop one day, anyway. It had stopped for the First.

The field was flooded. Everything was flooded. After the final blast, the water began to drain back into the river.

The world was quiet.

After a minute, I heard yelling. They were the voices of men. Only men.

Had the Legion been swallowed back through the Wound? I listened again. No shrieks or howls in my bad ear. Silence. Could it possibly be true?

I strained against the ground and climbed to my feet. *Abby?* I couldn't see her. I couldn't see much of anything. *Abby?* I thought I was calling out for her, but my mouth hadn't moved. My sneakers were gone, lost in the blast. My shirt was torn. I pushed my hair from my eyes and looked around the field.

"Abby?" I said, for real this time, but it was barely a whisper.

No answer.

I sloshed across the soggy ground. It was slow going without shoes. Sirens cut sharply through the air. I stumbled into a ditch, gagged on muddy water, and climbed to my feet again, taking longer this time.

"Abby!" My voice sounded like a little boy's voice.

She was nowhere in sight. I tried to unplug my ears. My bad ear was as dull as it had been before the crash.

Without the distracting howls, one clear thought rang in my head.

Find the First.

But there was no need to find him. He found me.

The woods burst with movement and he rushed at me, a nightmare of froth and rage. The white ghostly creature, boiling mad, galloped in on a wild horse. He was strapped into some kind of contraption made out of wicker and wood. Leather straps held him upright. His useless legs fluttered like fallen banners. Ulysses' saber waved in his skeletal hand.

I stumbled back. The horse's eyes were huge with fear as the First charged at me, hacking with the broken saber.

To translate into me? No, to cut me — any way he could.

My feet were stuck in the mud. I leaned away, fell to the ground, got up again. The mad horse wailed, and the First came at me again. I hustled toward the cover of the trees. It was so far. I heard the hooves behind me and dived into a flooded ditch, hoping the beast wouldn't trample me.

The horse twisted its legs in the mud and slid down to one knee. The First lurched forward, nearly out of his wicker saddle, within inches of me. I clawed my way out of the ditch and staggered into the trees.

There was a quick, small movement in the woods, and I was down again. My knee crunched on a fallen tree limb. This time, it was Waldo Fouks who'd knocked me down. He and the First had both gotten off the dredger before it had sunk.

Muttering, Waldo leaped onto my back, grasping at my neck, trying blindly to cut me. I tugged on the broken tree limb and swung it up out of the mud. It whacked Waldo on the shoulder. I sloughed him off and pressed deeper into the woods.

Where was Abby?

I ran along a path, but the First galloped up behind me. I fell again.

A shriek sounded behind me, and a cold hand gripped my arm. I turned.

It was Ronny. His face was a death mask. The patch of rot had spread to his nose and over his left eye.

The horse surprised him, rearing up. Its hooves clawed the air and knocked Ronny to the ground. He lay twisted and still in the water.

"Cut the boy!" the First yelled to Waldo. But Waldo hadn't caught up with us yet.

In a rage, I reached up and dragged the First off his horse. The whole saddle tumbled to the ground. The old man fell on me, a deadweight, arms flailing, saber slicing.

I pushed the broken blade away. He slashed at my leg. I fell back on my hands, crawled away, and staggered to my feet again. My eyes were flooded with swamp water. I grabbed a stone, pounded it at the old man wherever I could. He groaned, his gray head jutting backward. His neck was black.

He would die soon . . . or translate one more time.

Regaining his balance, the First swung the sword again, sliced my shirt, creased my stomach. There wasn't much blood — less each time I was cut.

"Ronny!" I cried, looking around frantically. "Ronny!"

"He's . . . dead," the First gargled.

I wouldn't believe it.

Sirens closed in. Fire trucks roared on the far side of the river. Voices wailed. Not ghost voices, not the Legion. Living people.

Maybe we had done enough. Maybe I should just let myself be cut, leave others to eliminate the dead who had survived the explosion.

Then Cane appeared, and I knew it was over. His dead face was half burned away from Ronny's attack on the barge.

Somehow Ronny stumbled to his feet then, eyes blazing, legs jerking like a puppet's. He wasn't dead, but he was close. His face was sliced open on one side. He fell on Cane from behind. They clawed at each other in the mud, each with the other's head in his arms.

One engine roared louder now.

The old hearse wove crazily through the trees. I could see Abby — Abby! — weeping behind the wheel. She drove straight at Waldo, thumping over the ditches, her face completely pale.

Waldo shrieked when he heard the hearse. He scrambled to get out of the way, but slipped and disappeared under its wheels. A burst of black air coiled up from the mud.

The First gave a weak yell from the ground nearby, and the horse rushed at me again. It knocked me to the ground. The old man grabbed its neck and was dragged into the trees, heading away from the river.

He had escaped.

Abby bolted from the hearse. "Ronny!"

I looked behind me. Cane and Ronny lay nearly motionless in the mud. Ronny's neck was turned in an awful way. He wrenched his arms once, and Cane cried out, digging his feet into the mud over and over until he went still. A wisp of black smoke coiled up from the back of Cane's head.

"Ronny!" I sank into the mud next to him. "Ronny, what can I do? Don't leave me! I'll find you someone, a new body —"

"No," he said, his voice broken. "I was w-w-wrong to tell you to translate your t-troops. I should have known you c-couldn't do that. The ghosts pushed the Legion into the w-water anyway. I saw it. You sent the Legion back. They're gone. The Wound is c-closed."

I couldn't speak.

Ronny's neck was still twisted, but his features eased. "Maybe I'll f-find my —Virgil's — family now. I'll fight if I have to. But maybe since we defeated the Legion here, things will get better there. Because of you, Derek."

"Ulysses, you mean," I said, my tears dripping onto his face.

"I mean Derek," he said firmly. "And hey, sorry I wasn't your real brother. . . ."

I was going to tell him he was wrong when he twitched all over. His head sank back. A coil of dark air flew up past me and away. I held him tight in my arms, but he was already as still as stone.

"Derek," Abby whispered. "I'm so . . ."

I stayed there for a while, then pulled away. There was practically nothing left of Ronny but a cold shell. Anyway, he had been wrong. Over the last few days we'd become as tight as brothers ever could be.

I felt empty. Abby hooked her arm through mine and leaned against me.

We heard a wail of pain and something else — the clang of metal. Together, we staggered through the pine trees and saw Dicky Meade's body, a dead husk, as white and dry as sand on the wet ground. The slice mark on the side of his head was like paper peeling off a wall. He'd found a new victim.

"The First is out there," said Abby. "In someone new."

The victim hadn't wanted to go. I could see the proof of a short but fierce struggle. Nearby, nearly buried in the mud, was a sword handle. Abby pulled it from the ground.

The broken saber.

"He'll want that back," I said softly.

"Let him try to get it. It belongs to you, anyway." She handed it to me.

I stood among the trees, holding my old saber, and let the heavy rain rush over me like a waterfall.

Abby touched my arm and turned to the car. "We need to get out of here," she said. "New Orleans. My family is there — what's left of it. Grammy Nora. You have Uncle Carl. My mother's out there. Your mother. And your dad, whoever he is. We'll pick up the pieces."

I listened to the sirens coming closer. The First was still here, but maybe Ronny had been right. With their leader — the First — on our side, and after this defeat, the Legion would be weaker in the afterlife. Maybe armies of the translated dead were a thing of the past. Maybe there was hope for peace in the other world. And in ours.

Maybe.

It was nice to think so.

I know one thing: The Wound is sealed shut. My ears tell me that. The Legion is gone. As impossible as it seems, Ronny and Abby and I have done it.

My mother once told me, *"The Legion will fall, the Wound will be closed, and life can return. Not for you, but for the others."*

Maybe not for me, but I'm still here. Maybe I'll discover why I bleed like the First, maybe not, but for now I'm still moving.

Who am I?

I'm Derek Stone. I'm Ulysses Longtemps.

I'm Derek Longtemps Stone.

Sirens coiled over everything now. Helicopters thudded. We needed to be out of there before the police descended on the field. They'd mop up this horrifying mess. They'd try to explain it. But that was all it would be: a possible explanation.

If you followed this story, you'll know better.

I turned to Abby. "Let the hearse finally do its job."

She looked at me as if she hoped to find something particular in my face. I don't know if she found it. She just nodded and helped me put Ronny into the back of the big car. She slumped into the driver's seat.

I slid in next to her.

"To New Orleans," she said. "The long way."

I picked up the battered road map, cupped my dead ear, and listened. Nothing. Good.

Abby let her eyes settle on me for a moment, then looked ahead and shoved the old car into gear, and we were gone. Home.

Goosebumps HorrorLand

SCHOLASTIC

www.EnterHorrorLand.com

GBH12SG